T0163146

Raven Wakes the World
A Winter Tale

Raven Wakes the World
A Winter Tale

By John Adcox
Illustrated by Carol Bales

THE
ST●RY
PLANT

The Story Plant
Studio Digital CT, LLC
P.O. Box 4331
Stamford, CT 06907

Text Copyright © 2020 by John Adcox
Illustrations Copyright © 2020 by Carol Bales

Story Plant hardcover ISBN-13: 978-1-61188-292-6
Fiction Studio Books e-book ISBN-13: 978-1-945839-48-1

Visit our website at www.TheStoryPlant.com

First Story Plant Printing: October 2020

Printed in the United States of America
0 9 8 7 6 5 4 3 2 1

For our parents

foreword

Way back in 2001, my friend Carol Bales (she wasn't yet my beloved wife) and I began the tradition of creating holiday gifts of story for our friends and family. I wrote a story; she created illustrations. We printed them and bound them by hand. At the time, our plan was to do a new one every year. We haven't quite accomplished that yet—since then, we've done a total of four. *Raven Wakes the World* was our very first collaboration. It was inspired by my own love of myth in all its many shapes and forms, and by Carol's stories of a friend who lives on an island in Alaska. I met Carol's friend years later, and she's absolutely nothing like the Katie in the story. I wasn't especially accurate with the island, either, but I suppose that's okay. I like to think the truths lurking in mythopoeia are of a different sort.

The story here has been expanded extensively from the original version, but Carol's illustrations are the same.

Since these stories started out as gifts, I'd like to thank our friends and family members for the blessings of their love and inspiration. Many thanks to James Lock, Bill Bridges, John Bridges, Nancy Fletcher, Ted Anderson, Sid "Bubba" Taylor, Zachary Steele, Jolie Simmons, and Andrew Greenberg for helping me polish this tale. I am especially grateful to Don Dudenhoeffer, Alice Neuhauser, Irtaza Barlas, and the whole Gramarye Media team for being great people and business partners. Thanks to Jim Meeks, Christina Kaylor, and Judith Pritchett for teaching me how to write (albeit when I probably should have been learning other things). Finally, I am forever grateful to James A. Moore, Ray Bradbury, Charles de Lint, Paul Brandon, and Lloyd Alexander for many kind words and much encouragement. Special thanks to Lou Aronica and Peter Miller for pushing me to lift this story higher.

Most of all, thanks to Carol, love of my life.

Carol and I wish you and yours the happiest of Winter Holiday Seasons, filled to the brim with bright music, warm welcomes and good company, the scent of roasted chestnuts and cinnamon treats piping from the oven, the taste of wine and chocolate, the cozy feel of hands cradling favorite mugs, laughter and merry toasts, blessings and numinous moments of the sacred, safe travels, and the light of stars and candles to guide you home.

"In the earliest time, when both people and animals lived on the earth, a person could become an animal if he wanted to and an animal could become a human being.

Sometimes they were people and sometimes animals and there was no difference. All spoke the same language.

That was the time when words were like magic. The human mind had mysterious powers. A word spoken by chance might have strange consequences.

It would suddenly come alive and what people wanted to happen could happen—all you had to do was to say it. Nobody can explain this: That's the way it was."

— Edward Field
Songs and Stories of the Netsilik Eskimos

1

All the World Was White

t was cold, and all the world was white.

Snow covered the stony island, and from where Katie Mason stood, the icy landscape blended into the overcast winter sky, white melding into frigid white, without shape, distance, or horizon. It was the white of a barren canvas, or fallow stone, art stillborn. The only change from the stunning, melancholy monotony of white was a single black bird, a large crow, or raven, maybe, that circled overhead once, twice, and three times before winging away over the still sea toward the frozen rocks of the mainland.

"I wish he'd stayed," Katie said aloud, her syllables disappearing in a cloud of frost. "I could use some damn company." The mist carried her words away, and then they were lost. She pulled her coat more tightly around her. She wished she'd worn a second shirt beneath her sweater. The wind had teeth. She didn't shiver; she was too numb for motion.

She should be moving, she knew that, but she stood still, like a statue shaped from ice. She'd planned to take the boat to the mainland and then drive into town. She would need supplies soon. Soon, nothing. She'd needed them yesterday. Coffee and wine, food and paint. Well, not paint, not really. She had plenty of paint.

She really should start moving. Down to the boat, across to the truck. One step, then another. Who knew? Maybe the new chisel set she'd ordered would be in. Maybe if she had the new tools, the novelty would spark excitement and the excitement would flare into passion. Passion. That's what she needed. Then maybe she'd be able to sculpt again.

Maybe.

But it was so cold, so terribly cold, and the wind reached through her heaviest coat and sweaters to chill her blood and frost the very marrow of her bones.

Maybe it would be warmer tomorrow.

Yes, tomorrow would be soon enough. She could go into town then.

She went back inside.

The cabin's great room was to have been her studio. After all, she'd come all the way up here to Alaska, to the very end of the world, to work. To work and to heal. As a studio space, it should have been perfect. It was quiet; the room was large and airy, at least by local standards; and the windows looked to the east. They were small, true, but when there was light, they let it in. The overheads were white but not too harsh, and they cast few shadows. Her tools and brushes were arranged just the way she liked them. The room had no sink, but that was okay. The kitchen waited just through the door, and the sink there was a giant steel industrial one. Katie didn't mind walking a little while she worked. She hadn't used to, anyway.

She hadn't done any work, though, nothing more than a few false starts and aborted attempts. Here and there the projects she'd begun, or planned to, waited, still lost in barren stone or empty canvas. Sheets of glacier-white canvas stretched in frames glared accusations at her. Blocks of stone and plaster with just a few chips chiseled away lingered, children neither born nor aborted: the shapes and form of the art still frozen in slabs of unmoving white.

Only one showed any recognizable sign of creation at all: she'd begun a statue, but her effort had revealed only a single arm, fingers curled and grasping, like the limb of a drowning man reaching desperately for life from beneath the surface of an ice-covered northern sea. Katie stood still and looked at it for a long time. She should work on that one, she decided. Or something, anyway. She needed to work. When she was making, she wasn't thinking about Billy.

Katie sat down at a worktable, one where the sunlight was more or less good even in the Alaska winter. It would be pale bright for a little while longer. But she only gazed at the white marble, studying the swirls and textures like the ink in a Rorschach blot. The shapes hidden within eluded her; she could not free them from the stillness of stone. She never even reached for a tool.

So paint then, dammit, she commanded herself. *You're a bloody artist; bloody create something.*

She didn't bother with any of the efforts she'd started before. Instead, she stretched a new canvas and put up a frame. When she finished, when it was ready for her at last, she saw that it was white and pure and perfect, like a field of new snow, so very lovely in its desolate, pristine emptiness. She couldn't bring herself to touch it, to spoil its empty virgin-ice perfection.

Her heart was numb. If only it weren't so cold....

An hour passed before she gave up. She poured herself a mug of Irish Mist, pulled her favorite chair to the window where she could catch the last of the dim, fading, fatal light, and stared at the pages of a book. She tried not to think about Billy. After two more Irish Mists, she almost succeeded. That much, at least, was good. If she wasn't healing, at least she wasn't hurting. The pain lay still, numb in her breast. That was enough. When night came, she went to bed.

After three more days, she found herself out of everything. She'd finished the last of the milk more than a week ago. The bottles of wine and Irish Mist were empty. Even the last can of Spaghetti-Os was gone. Katie hated Spaghetti-Os. She'd purchased the cans out of habit; she used to keep them in the house for Billy.

"I like the kind with meatballs," he'd said one time as he helped her unpack her plastic bags. Katie had done the shopping in those days. Billy didn't like to go to the store, not even the new Stop & Shop with the scan-it-yourself checkout lanes. He said it embarrassed him to be there when she paid for everything, because he never had any money. Katie thought it made him feel, well, humiliated that she had money, even though he never actually said so, and even though she never had very much—especially not when shared by two.

"Your stuff's so much more *commercial* than mine," he'd told her. "My art confronts people. You know? Yeah. It's like a punch—" He slapped his left palm with his right fist for emphasis. "—smack! Right in the gut. You know? It makes them uncomfortable. That's why they don't buy it."

"Maybe if you finish your series," Katie had suggested softly. "Do your show. Right, baby? Let them, just, *see*—"

Billy looked at her and rolled his eyes. "I'm not commercial. I'm not like you. I'm moved by a muse, not by money. Muses don't work on goddamn deadlines, you know. Christ, Babe, what's wrong with you? Why can't you even *see* that?"

Katie had felt very small. He'd tried to be gentle, but she'd heard the accusation in his voice. And the contempt. Just like when he'd unpacked the Spaghetti-Os.

"They were out of the meatball ones, honey," Katie had explained. "I looked. Okay? Look. I got the ones with little hot dogs. Can't you eat those? Just this once? Or here. Let me make us something."

Billy hadn't answered.

"Baby, I did my best. Okay? Maybe you can come with me next time. Then you can pick out what you like. Okay?"

"Honestly, Katie. Sometimes I think you do these things just to belittle me." He'd shook his head and walked away. He'd sulked for the rest of the week.

That was before, a lifetime ago. Billy was gone now, and she was in Alaska, and she'd still bought the stupid cans, the ones with meatballs.

Now even they were gone.

So was the last of the coffee.

Worse, the roof had started to leak again, and snow whirled in to settle like dust on the cold stones and barren canvases she hadn't even begun to make into art.

2

The Memory of a Winter Dream

fter two more days, Katie finally went to town—Aurora, Alaska, nestled just a few miles north and inland from the last port where the cruises called. A few of the braver tourists looking for the true northern adventure made their way there, so the town obliged them by putting up authentic Alaskan wilderness lodges, complete with Jacuzzis and steak houses, and a few shops and galleries selling authentic Eskimo art and crafts, some of it actually made by Inuit Native Americans.

Already decked out in its holiday finery, Aurora displayed itself like a toy village in a crystal snow globe, or a town in a Christmas card, or the memory of a winter dream too bright and lovely to be real. Katie couldn't help but gasp and smile at the wonder of the town's winter charm as she pulled into the parking lot across from Tallbear's General Store and Gallery. The few spaces there were full, so she pulled out to find a spot along the street.

Main Street detoured around the Aurora town square. There, the tall pine in the center twinkled with sparkling color, silver and gold, and a bright galaxy of delicate ornaments hung shining beneath a star blazing on the highest bough. Every shop, building, and lamppost along Main Street had been decorated with garlands of greenery and sparkling white lights, and the windows and doorways wore proud red ribbons beneath wreaths and blinking electric candles. Winter contributed, too; every single bow, bough, and ornament was dusted with snow and hung with icicles.

Only the occasional spots of coal black, interspersed in shop windows, doorways, and even on the Christmas tree, seemed oddly out of place, at least to Katie's artist's eye. As she passed, she looked closer. All of the night black figures were stylized ravens set among the golden angels and jolly snowmen. She braked, wiped the frost away from her side window with her mitten, and looked again. Her brow crinkled.

Ravens?

Shaking her head, Katie drove on. A little further ahead, she found a parking place on Main Street, right in front of a row of shops across and two short blocks down from Tallbear's General Store. Tallbear's was her destination, but Katie lingered, walking slowly, looking in the windows of the souvenir galleries. Rows of tiny carvings, stone fetishes, looked back at her. Were those Inuit? Katie had seen them back in Boston. Katie wondered what the artists had thought as they crafted them. Had they felt totem spirits stirring in the unshaped rock, waiting to be freed? Or were they just filling orders, crafting myth forms like crystal unicorns simply to make a few dollars? In the back of her mind, she heard Billy sniff derisively. *Commercial.*

Behind them, Katie saw a display of paintings, tall canvases depicting winter scenes in acrylic, oil, and watercolor. When she turned her head to the side, she thought she could see animal shapes lurking in the shadows and forms of line and color where sea met rock and ice. Had the artist placed them there? Or were they simply tricks of light and imagination? She found herself rather hoping the latter. It would be good to be imagining things again. Her mind had been cold for a long time.

The next window featured watercolors of Alaska natives—stern, dark-eyed faces in winter gear, few of them smiling. Katie frowned. The other shop had been better. The art in Tallbear's would be better still, light years better. But people bought the pictures here just the same. She saw a couple making a purchase even as she watched.

I could sell here, Katie told herself. *I could make a living.*

When she'd first come to Aurora, she'd sold two paintings and a bust. They were all of Billy. She had no idea why she'd brought them along; she'd come here to forget, to heal—to leave the relationship and its bitter, broken end behind. When Maggie Tallbear offered to display them in the gallery adjoining her shop, she'd jumped at the chance. When they'd sold, she'd been delighted. Thrilled, even. But she'd created those three pieces long ago, in summer: a time of warmth and smiles when the world was green, except when the last light turned it to softly shining gold.

She'd missed the pieces at first; the empty places were like missing teeth that she kept probing with her tongue, even when she told herself not to. But over time, the pain chilled to a dull numbness deep in the belly, a hollow place in heart and womb.

Mrs. Tallbear had asked for more, more than once, but Katie hadn't made anything new in months. It was winter now, and cold. Over time, the bubbling excitement had numbed to apathy.

Maybe in the spring, she thought. Things would thaw then, and it wouldn't be so awfully, achingly cold.

She chewed her lower lip, which was chapped in the cold wind. The couple left with their wrapped package, laughing and touching. They were from out of town; already, Katie had been in Aurora long enough to spot the tourists. They looked happy. *Why on Earth would happy people come here?* she wondered. *Why would they come all the way to the end of the world, where it's so damn cold?*

For a long moment, she didn't move. She looked at the art in the frosted windows even after she'd stopped seeing it. At last—after a few minutes or several, she couldn't have guessed how many—she shook her head. *Enough,* she told herself. She had errands.

Holding her coat closed against the wind and snow, she hurried across the street to Tallbear's. Silver bells jingled as she opened the door and slipped inside. She found the store surprisingly crowded. Mrs. Tallbear hurried this way and that to deal with customers while a line of tourists waited in front of the register.

Katie shuddered. Crowds, even small ones, unnerved her. They always had, even when she'd had to go to the Stop & Shop for Billy's Spaghetti-Os, but especially lately. She waited for a few minutes, standing still and trying to make herself small.

Katie's stomach rumbled; she was hungry, she realized. She should eat something. Didn't they always say never to shop for groceries when you're hungry? She could always come back to the store later. *Christ, later, yes,* when the crowd was gone. She glanced at her watch. The pub should be open; she didn't think it closed between lunch and dinner like some of the other places. She decided to go have a bite. Why not? She could be listless at the pub as well as she could anywhere else. Maybe when she returned, the store would be empty.

Besides, the diversion would delay Maggie Tallbear's inevitable questions about her art—for a little while, anyway. Plus, if she ate in town, her groceries would last one lunch longer. That would make one more day before she had to trudge all the way back to Aurora for more supplies. Which meant one more day in which she might actually make something for Mrs. Tallbear's shop. And if she didn't, well, that meant one more day before she'd have to face her disappointed, reproving gaze again.

The snow fell harder as she left the shop to walk beneath constellations of twinkling Christmas lights that crisscrossed over the street on wires, while an unkindness of ravens danced and twirled all around her, a swirling maelstrom of black and frozen white.

Sam's Old Stonewall Pub was just a block or two away.

Wasn't it?

For a moment, Katie stopped and turned around, disoriented. She looked one way, then the other. In the snow, the streets looked the same. Choosing a direction more or less at random, she cut down an alley and across a snow-covered parking lot. She frowned. Shouldn't the pub be here?

Had she made a wrong turn? How could she? Aurora only had six streets!

But no, there it was, just around the corner, a few doors down. She'd missed the chalkboard specials menu (which hadn't changed in decades) and the wooden sign both in the snow. The cold numbed her cheek and bleached away the last of her blush. Katie hurried across and pushed the heavy oaken door open. She closed her eyes and breathed, relieved to escape the blasting cold and the optical overload of dervishing snow and spinning color as she stepped into the pub's dark warmth. She closed the door firmly behind her, hushing the wind.

This late in the afternoon, most of the lunch crowd had gone. New Sam himself stood behind the bar, chatting with the only other customer as he finished a steaming bowl of Sam's special chili and a mug of foamy red ale. New Sam's name wasn't really Sam; it was Jim. But the pub's name was Sam's, and the pub was his. Nor was there anything apparently new about the swarthy-faced, white-haired, long-bearded old man. But the Aurora locals started calling him New Sam as soon as he took over running the pub from his grandfather, the first Sam. All these long winters later, everyone still called him New Sam, even after most of them had long since forgotten why.

Katie sat down on the last stool at the other end of the bar, the one farthest from the other customer. It was also farthest from the fireplace, but that didn't bother her. Even at the distance, the warmth from the crackling little blaze melted away the ice from her buttons and brought life back to her cold fingers, enough so that she could pull off her coat. Once free, she placed it carefully on the stool next to her. The cold reached her again, but it wasn't as bad. She hardly noticed it anymore. Cold had become a part of her; her heart's blood was frost and warmth was a long-ago, unfamiliar thing.

She felt very small on the big stool. That feeling, that sudden sensation of intense smallness, coupled with her hunger to make her feel altogether insubstantial. She felt light, like a ghost; like a cloud that might drift away with the merest puff of bitter winter wind, to be lost forever in snow and sky. A part of her liked that idea: to escape, to see the world from above, distant and small, like a painting hung too far away to see its individual brushstrokes; to study it from on high before she disappeared into endless, empty blue. She didn't float away, though. Instead, she studied the menu spelled out neatly on the chalkboard behind the bar.

"Don't bother with that," New Sam told her with a smile.

For a moment, Katie panicked. She'd forgotten he could see her. She was a woman, not a spirit or a cloud.

"All we have is chili," New Sam continued. "And all my pots and pans are in the washer. So there's nothing else 'til dinner time." He shrugged. "So it's chili or wait a couple hours."

Katie frowned. *Chili?* She'd planned on something lighter, like a salad, maybe, even though she hadn't eaten anything more than crackers in a day or two. But chili! Chili was so . . . substantial. It was fire that made her legs heavy and anchored her to the ground, like stone, bones of the world, or the roots of a tree.

"It's really good chili."

Katie looked around, startled. The other customer, the man at the end of the bar, had spoken. He smiled at her.

"Sorry," he said. "Didn't mean to make you jump. But it *is* good chili. Warm and hearty. Good and spicy but not too hot. Peppery. No beans to ruin it."

Katie looked over at the man, giving him more than a glance for the first time. At once, her artist's eye began to stir. His hair fell long and straight and shiny black, framing native Inuit features. But his face wasn't round like most of the locals'. It was long and sharp, a face of edge and angles, and his eyes were a deep and bright black, like the patches of sky between stars. For a moment, Katie wished she had a sketchbook. She longed to capture that face, to hold it, to make it into art. It was a feeling she'd almost forgotten; she hadn't experienced it since Billy. She looked quickly away.

"I can add some beans if you want 'em," said New Sam. "Got a pot going, with a little chili juice to flavor 'em. If you need beans, that is."

"Better without them," the other customer said. "But have New Sam here add you some cheddar."

"I'll have the chili," she said softly.

"Beans?" New Sam asked.

"No, thank you," said Katie.

"Good choice," said New Sam with a nod.

"Don't forget the cheddar," the other customer suggested.

"The cheddar comes with," said New Sam. "You can sprinkle it on or not. Up to you. Want something to drink?"

"Um . . . what?" So many choices, so many questions to answer! Katie had been on her own for a long time. She'd forgotten what it was like, the frenetic vibrancy of even the simplest casual human contact. She'd forgotten how many demands there were in conversation with strangers. She longed for the familiar comfort of solitude. She wished she could be home again with a blanket. She wished she could curl up in a cocoon and sleep.

"You seem a little lightheaded," New Sam said, not unkindly. "So maybe not a beer, eh? Not on an empty stomach. I've got sodas or water. How about that? Or hey, how about some coffee? The coffee's good."

"No it's not," said the man at the end of the bar.

"It's hot," New Sam said defensively.

"It oughta be," the other man said with a grin. "It's been on the stove since, what? Yesterday? Last week?"

The man was handsome, Katie noticed. He was lean and strong, like Billy. But this man liked to grin: the smile was as much a part of him as the color of his eyes. She wondered what Billy would have looked like if he'd smiled more. It probably would have ruined the sullen, bitter artist look he cultivated so carefully, she decided. Since he'd never actually produced anything in the time they'd been together, that moody, cynical persona was just about all that let him hang on to his claim of being an artist.

"How long's that brew been cooking, anyhow?"

The man's words snapped her thoughts away from Billy and the past. She was glad. The pain had begun to creep up on her again, a little anyway, and she felt suddenly warm.

"Since lunch time," Sam said. He glared and shook his finger at the other man. "Now hush up, Luke. You're going to drive my customer away."

"Besides," said the man, "hot coffee's no good with hot chili. You need something cool. Cool and hot together, that's just the thing. Like the cheddar."

He wasn't just handsome, Katie decided. No, he was more than just handsome. He was beautiful.

"Opposites are always best, aren't they?" He seemed to expect an answer, but Katie didn't know what to say. "That's why twilight's the prettiest time of day. Isn't it? When the sky turns that deep purple color. You know. It's night and day all mixed together, like a potion. But hey, don't listen to me. I'm keeping you from ordering."

"I'll have water." Katie looked down again.

"Coming up," said New Sam. He disappeared back into the kitchen area behind the bar.

"Hi," said the other man.

Katie looked up, startled. "What?"

The man smiled again, still looking at her.

"Hi," he repeated. His smile widened. "Here, I've been helping you order your lunch and all, and I haven't even said hello."

"Um, hello." Katie was confused. The man seemed to want something from her. Didn't he? Why else would he talk to her? Why couldn't he just let her be insubstantial? Couldn't he see that she wanted to float away like winter mist?

"I'm Lucas Tulukkam," the man said. God, but he was beautiful. No man had any right to be that beautiful.

"I'm Katie Mason," she said, a sound something between a squeak and a whisper, when her voice returned to her. Her blush made her cheeks warm.

New Sam brought her a tall glass of water without ice and a bowl of steaming chili with cheddar on the side and a hunk of warm bread.

"The bread's fresh," New Sam promised. "Just made a few loaves for the dinner crowd."

Katie ate some of the chili, trying it both with and without the cheese, and nibbled at the bread, then paid her tab as fast as she could. She didn't wait for her change. She didn't look back at Lucas, either, nor did she answer when he called out a friendly, "See you later, Katie!"

She hurried away and escaped back into the cold, where the wind and snow numbed her to calmness again.

3

Long Ago There Was No Light in the World, and the People Lived in Cold and Darkness

ust as she'd hoped, Katie found the general store emptier when she returned. Maggie Tallbear was chatting with a lingering customer, but she smiled and waved when she saw Katie. "Be with you in a minute, Hon," she called. "Pour yourself a cuppa and get comfortable, okay? The tea things are there on the little table by the window."

Katie filled a mug and sweetened it with honey and milk. She wished she had a shot of whiskey to spice it with; the warmth of alcohol going down would numb her as surely as the cold. There wasn't any, so she made do.

She didn't sit, though. While Mrs. Tallbear fussed with the other customer, Katie wandered up and down the cramped aisles, filling a basket with groceries. She didn't know why she bothered with the basket. She needed to buy more than it would hold, as much as her truck and boat would carry. She had a big freezer, after all, and if she happened to fill it before she put everything away, well, what the hell. Her island was one big freezer.

Tallbear's wasn't like the Stop & Shop back home. Only seven rows were devoted to groceries. Katie found that comforting. With fewer choices, she didn't have to think as much. Her mind could rest, numb and comfortable. She didn't really notice what she put into her basket; she simply picked out what she hoped would be enough to last a couple of months. That way, she reminded herself again, she wouldn't have to come all the way back to town as soon. Maybe then she'd get some work done. Besides, everything tasted pretty much the same lately. She passed the Spaghetti-O's—those tinned reminders of all the burning pain she'd fled Boston to escape, to forget—but she only glanced at the cans before passing them by. It felt both strange and satisfying.

When her basket was full, Katie emptied it on the counter by the register and went to fill it again. Four or five baskets full ought to do it. She knew she should be checking the prices, but she didn't bother. Thanks largely to the legacy her grandmother had left her, her savings would last for years if she was frugal, or even if she wasn't especially. Living was cheap in Aurora.

As she wandered back to the grocery aisles, she took a peek in the shop's other room, the gallery. Most of the current stock was geared to the coming Christmas holiday—the community's local artists and craftspeople knew how to please the tourists. There were also ravens. Lots of them. An unkindness of ravens.

"Hey there," Mrs. Tallbear said at last. The old woman's voice startled Katie. "Sorry, didn't mean to make you jump. Did I leave you waiting too long?"

Maggie Tallbear was a short woman, smaller than Katie's own 5'2", plump but not fat. She had a round face and braids, black streaked with silver, hanging down to her waist. She wasn't always smiling, but the crow's feet at the sides of her wise, dark eyes made it look as if she were always just about to.

"No, no," Katie said, blushing slightly. "I just finished picking out my stuff."

"I don't suppose you brought me anything?" Mrs. Tallbear asked hopefully, her eyebrows arching high on her forehead.

"No," Katie admitted. She found it hard to meet the woman's dark eyes, so she looked away, back to the crafts in the gallery room, back to the Christmas decorations and the black ravens.

"Pity. I could use some real art to go with all the touristy knickknack crap my locals are turning out these days."

"Some of it's really good."

"Most of it is. You know what I mean."

"I'll try to do something soon."

"That's what you said last time."

"Well, I did. Try, I mean."

"Been busy?"

"It's winter," Katie hedged.

Mrs. Tallbear nodded. "Yes, there's always a lot to do in winter, isn't there? And spring and summer, too, not to mention fall."

"I suppose."

"So what have you started on? Painting? Sculpture?"

Katie shrugged. "I haven't been working too much," she admitted.

"Really? I thought that's why you came up here. To work, I mean."

Katie shrugged again. "And to heal a little."

"Ah, yes. I see. And how's that coming?"

"This helps," Katie said, smiling and pointing to the bottles of red wine and Irish Mist in her basket.

Mrs. Tallbear frowned. "That make you feel better?"

"It makes me feel nothing."

"That's not the same thing," Mrs. Tallbear pointed out.

"I'll take what I can get."

"And that's the best idea, then?"

Katie looked away and changed the subject. "What's with all the ravens? Not exactly Christmassy, are they?"

"Oh, they are up here."

"Seriously?"

"Be a lot of trouble to find all these ravens if I was making a joke, wouldn't it?"

"I suppose so. So, what's the deal?"

"Don't tell me you don't know about Raven? And the festival?"

"'Fraid not."

"The celebration of Raven happens every year, 'round the end of December. Why, up here in Alaska, it's just about as big as Christmas!"

"I guess I missed it."

"Well, it's quite the to-do! You'll get to know old Raven this year for sure."

"What's it about?"

"Well, it's a story, sacred to my people," said Mrs. Tallbear. "Most of the people around here have all turned Christian, but you can bet they still celebrate the Raven!"

"So . . . this Raven's, what, like, special to the Inuit people?"

Mrs. Tallbear nodded. "To people all over the world, even to you white people. Those who remember it, anyway. In Scotland, people who have the Raven's knowledge are supposed to have supernatural insight. Couple tourists told me that a few seasons back. Got all excited to tell New Sam—his mother was Scottish, you know—

but it turned out he already knew. How about that? Why, people all over know about Raven. Odin up north and Apollo way down in Greece traveled with ravens. Not that I know all that much about them, mind. Odin and Apollo, I mean."

"So, uh, what does it have to do with Christmas? Did a raven, like, visit baby Jesus?"

Mrs. Tallbear pursed her lips as she considered.

"Probably," she said at last, nodding. "That's not it, though. But it *is* about a baby born to a virgin in winter, and light shining in a dark world. That's sure Christmas-sy, isn't it?"

"Gosh, that's a *lot* like the Christmas story. I mean, like straight out of Sunday School. That's kind of weird, isn't it?"

"I don't see why," said Mrs. Tallbear. "I'd think an event as significant as the birth of God himself as a baby here on Earth would be so powerful that it would be just bound to have echoes in every culture there is, and resonance in every corner of the world. Wouldn't you? Why, even all the way up here in Alaska! And yes, even before the white Europeans came. It's an old, old story."

"Tell me?"

"Of course, dear. Here, now. Why don't we sit down at the table? Just leave your things there by the register; they'll be okay. Don't mind the cold stuff; it's close enough to the door. It'll be chilly enough. That's better. Now then. I'll tell you all about it. Wait, here, let me get you some more tea. Take yours with honey? Right, of course you do."

Katie watched the snow through the frosted window while Mrs. Tallbear puttered around, whistling happily. A stylized raven mounted on a telephone pole, along with a green wreath with red berries, kept a lookout on the street below. Katie stood for a better view and tried to imagine the painted black bird in Scotland or Greece. She tilted her head and chewed her lower lip.

When the mugs were filled and steaming, the women sat back down comfortably at the table by the window. Mrs. Tallbear took a sip, but the tea was still too hot, so she put down her mug and began her tale.

"Long ago there was no light in the world, and the people lived in cold and darkness. Raven looked down, and he saw that the people were unhappy in the cold, eternal shadow. Raven likes bright, shiny things, so he felt real sorry for all the people in the dark land."

"Just . . . Raven? I mean, not like one particular one?"

"*The* Raven. The first Raven, oldest of all. The grandfather Raven. My great aunt used to say that Raven had already forgotten more than whole nations ever know long before old Eve munched her old snake-polished red apple. 'Course, I don't know if that's true."

"I see."

"Now, Raven, he knew that way up in the sky was a great house where a selfish old chief kept all the light to himself. The chief wouldn't share the light, because he only loved himself. Himself and his only child, a beautiful daughter. This is a true story, you know."

Katie lifted an eyebrow. "It is?"

Mrs. Tallbear nodded. "It's been told by grandfather to granddaughter and grandmother to grandson since the beginning of time. What can be truer than that?" She stirred her tea, blew on it to cool it, and took a sip. Satisfied that it was both cool and sweet enough, she nodded and took another sip before continuing her tale.

"Now, one day, Raven found the selfish chief's daughter alone at the river, gathering water to drink. She was very beautiful, you know."

Katie nodded. "You said."

"So I did. I think Raven loved her. He likes shiny things, and nothing shines like a beautiful young girl."

"Wait a minute. How could a raven love a girl?"

"Not *a* raven. *The* Raven. Things are different with the first spirits, the oldest ones. And Raven, why, he's the oldest mystery of all."

"I see," said Katie, even though she didn't.

"So Raven, he turned himself into a tiny berry and floated down to where she knelt by the water. The girl drank the water, and as she did, she swallowed the berry that was Raven. Now, that berry was a seed, sure enough. Soon, that seed began to grow in her belly. Nine months later, the time came for her to have her baby. As was customary, they made a hole for her, in which she was to give birth."

Katie frowned. "She was supposed to give birth in a hole?"

"That's what they did back then," Mrs. Tallbear explained with a nod. "It was a long time ago, like I said. Anyway, they lined that hole with furs and brightly woven cloth. But the baby wouldn't come. He didn't want to be born in such fine things. Well, the selfish chief, he loved his daughter, so he said, 'What shall we put in the hole?' They tried all sorts of things, and at last when they lined it with soft moss, the baby was happy and was born. The baby was tiny and beautiful, with night-black hair and eyes that were bright and quick. That baby was Raven in disguise."

"So he didn't look like a bird?"

"He looked like a baby, pink and fat and squawking."

The bells above the door jangled as two customers came in, interrupting the tale. Mrs. Tallbear went to greet them, but Katie took care not to make eye contact. In Aurora, eye contact was an invitation to friendly hellos and chats; Katie preferred to be quiet, anonymous. Not because she wanted to be unfriendly, oh, certainly not. But talking with strangers required energy that disturbed her carefully sheltered lethargy and made her open the social parts of her brain, parts that had been closed and tucked away in memory's dark attic, under a blanket of complacent numbness. She wasn't ready to start opening closed doors. *Oh, God, no.* Not yet.

Another customer came in just as the first two were leaving, and Katie concentrated on making herself small and silent: like a mouse, like a snowflake. She filled her basket twice more. When the shop emptied again at last, Mrs. Tallbear poured them each another mug.

"Now, then," she said as she stirred in generous spoons-ful of honey, "where was I?"

"The baby was just born," Katie reminded her. "The baby who was Raven in disguise."

"Right. Of course. Let's see, then." Mrs. Tallbear blew into her mug and took another sip. "Well, after a time, the baby started crying. His mother, and even his selfish old grandfather, tried everything they could think of to comfort the child. They tried rattles and hugs and blankets and food. They cooed; they made funny faces. Nothing worked. That little baby just kept right on crying, night and day. He kept on crying, crying and waving at one of the bundles that hung on the walls of the lodge. Finally, the chief said, 'Give my grandson what he is crying for. Give him that bundle on the end!' His daughter did so, and that was the bag of stars."

"Wait a minute," said Katie. "The stars? The stars were in a bag? All of them?"

Mrs. Tallbear nodded again. "All the stars were in that bag, the one the chief's daughter gave to baby Raven. Raven likes shiny things. But I told you that, didn't I? Of course I did. Would you like a cookie?"

"No, thanks."

"They're gingerbread. For Christmas, dear. All perfect-ly warm and very yummy!"

"No, thanks," Katie said again. She smiled. "Really."

"Suit yourself. I could probably do without them myself, I suppose. Anyway, the story.

"The baby Raven played with the bag of stars. He rolled them this way and that, until at last he rolled the bag over to the smoke hole, and then he let them go. Those stars, they all danced away, every last sparkling one of them, and they flashed off right into the sky. There they formed the patterns you see at night. It's the same dance of the stars, free and spinning in their places, still shining in those very same pictures to this very day. And all because of Raven and his mischief."

Katie smiled. "That's lovely."

Mrs. Tallbear nodded. "But now the baby had nothing to play with. So he cried, and cried again, and nothing his mother or the chief could do could comfort him. Finally, the old chief said, 'Give him something else to play with! Anything to quiet down that poor child. Give him another one of those bundles!' His daughter did so, and this was the bundle that contained the moon. Baby Raven played with it for a while, bouncing it like a ball, and he filled the lodge with silver light. At last he let it go, too, right out the smoke hole, and the moon took its place in the sky. And from there she still watches over us at night to this very day."

"Did the baby start crying again?"

"You're learning!"

Katie blushed and smiled.

"Once again that little baby started up crying," Mrs. Tallbear continued. "He cried so much they were afraid he would die! But the selfish old chief loved the baby boy as much as he loved his daughter, so once again he said, 'Give him that last bundle! Take it down and give it to him!'

"The daughter gave her baby the last bundle, the one that contained the sun. Now he had all the light. He cried out a great *Ga!* Then he turned back into Raven, and flew away through the smoke hole, taking the sun with him. When he reached the sky, why he let it go. It was too hot for him, even though he liked shiny things. He always has; he always will. The old chief was furious—why, he very nearly shook with hot, red rage, but there was nothing he could do. The sun took its place in the sky. And so Raven brought light to the world."

Katie smiled.

"That's lovely," she said again. She took another sip of tea. It was still deliciously hot. "I like that story."

"That's not the end," said Mrs. Tallbear. "Now there was *too much* light. It was light all the time, and soon the world got tired. Things grew all the time, shooting up wild as you please, why, without ever stopping even for a minute, and the people never slept. There was no rest. There was too much, too much light. So Raven took the light away for a while, and now there was night and day. But the world was still tired, so Raven took the sun far away. The first winter came, and with the cold and dark, the world slept. When the world had rested enough, Raven flew out to Sikrinaktok Island."

"Hey, I know that place. It's not far from my island!"

"It's the same," Mrs. Tallbear agreed with a nod. "So say the old people. From there, Raven cried out to the sun, and called him back. And sure enough, the sun started his journey back. Soon spring came to the world, and the world woke up from its long slumber. Now, every year, the sun goes away for a while so the Earth can rest."

"And Raven waits around until it's time to wake it up again."

"Raven? Ha! No, not Raven. He's a restless spirit, that one. He likes to travel around and play tricks. While the sun's gone, Raven wanders the world. Sometimes he visits the first spirits, the Old Mysteries. Sometimes he visits the animals, and when he does, he takes their shapes and lives among them. Sometimes Raven visits people, to see what the humans are up to. And when he does, he disguises himself as a man. But always, he has to come back so he can call back the sun and wake the world up again. He does it at midwinter. That's when the days start getting long again, you know."

"I see."

"Now sometimes, Raven forgets who he is."

Katie shook her head. "What do you mean?"

"He forgets he's Raven, doesn't he? He forgets he's got a job to do. He thinks he's just a man, or a squirrel, or a bear, or whatever he happens to be. Old Raven, he's got a big heart, sure, but he's easily distracted, you know? He finds something shiny that catches his attention, or he gets caught up in his games and tricks. When that happens, why, winter can drag on too long!"

"That's not good."

"Not good at all," Mrs. Tallbear agreed with a nod. She finished the last of her tea. "So each year at midwinter, all the people hang up shiny decorations, all the silver and gold things that Raven loves the best. All the bright things catch Raven's attention and remind him who he is, and what he has to do. Old Raven's also supposed to be something of a glutton, and they say even the simplest meals become feasts when he's around. That's why we put out such great spreads of food at this time of the year. Why, everyone loves a winter feast, don't they? Of course they do. Even that old rascal Raven. That attracts his attention too. The food and the light and the shining things, they remind him. And so, every year, Raven goes to Sikrinaktok Island and calls the sun. Raven wakes the world. Spring comes. That's why we have the Raven celebration to this very day."

"What a wonderful story!" said Katie.

"I'm glad you like it," said Mrs. Tallbear. "Of course, they tell it better than that at the festival."

"I doubt that."

"You're kind. But at the festival, why all the best sto-rytellers participate. And there's music, and dancing, and the drums . . . all the bright costumes with their feathers and masks. . . ."

"It sounds lovely."

Mrs. Tallbear nodded and pursed her lips thought-fully. "Maybe—"

Mrs. Tallbear didn't get to finish her thought. Just then, two more customers came in, and once again the woman was a whirlwind of activity as she hurried around to find them everything they needed. Katie finished her tea and made her way back to the register to pay for her purchases.

"This be all, dear?" Mrs. Tallbear asked when it was Katie's turn at last.

"I think so," she said. "Oh, unless you know what kind of stuff I need to fix my roof. The snow's coming in."

"Oh, crap. Is it leaking again?"

"A little."

"Well, don't worry. I'll find a handyman who can fix it right up and send him over to have a look. And don't worry," she added with a friendly wink, "I'll be sure your landlord gets the bill, not you."

"Thanks. I'd really appreciate that."

"My pleasure," said Mrs. Tallbear with a smile. "I'll find someone who's good and reputable, and send them right along, okay?"

Katie nodded. "Thank you. That'd be great. If it's no trouble."

"Not even a whit of it. Well, it might be a minute. Everyone'll be preparing for the big snow, but I'll get someone up there as fast as I can, don't you worry. Now, then. That everything?"

"That's it. Oh, wait. Did that chisel set I ordered come in?"

"I haven't seen it," Mrs. Tallbear said. "But I have a whole stack of deliveries in the back that I haven't even started going through. I can look right now if you'll wait a bit."

"I don't want to be any trouble. . . ."

"It's no trouble at all. Besides, this'll help you work, right?"

Katie looked down at the floor. She didn't answer. While Mrs. Tallbear went to check her deliveries, Katie started carrying loads of groceries back to her truck.

4

White and Changeless

he chisel set had arrived indeed, but inspiration hadn't come with it. Three days passed, white and changeless, and Katie hadn't even opened it. She almost had, three times now. She'd even gone so far as to carry it into the studio. She'd looked at the blocks of stone and plaster, all of them waiting for her touch to free the shapes trapped and frozen within, but in the end, she'd left them alone. The chisel set remained sealed and pristine.

An idea for a painting came to her, a winter scene like the view of the mainland she had from her back porch, but with elements of the fantastic culled from the depths of her own imagination. There would be bears, white and rolling like the sea, or like constellations with coats of stars, cold and blazing and distant. And people, frozen people dressed in leather and white fur, people with frost for blood and hearts of ice. They would carry enchantment about them, like halos, or auroras, made of light and whirling snow.

She stretched the canvas, and laid down a base coat, an even, pale blue. Next, she dipped her brush into a second color: white, pure and cold. She stirred it for a moment, looking for patterns in the whirling white. She didn't do anything else, though. She added neither form nor warmth of color. She left the brush on her white palette without even bothering to clean it. The excitement of inspiration died stillborn, frozen in her breast. Soon she forgot what she'd set out to capture. The creative fire was doused, so she abandoned the canvas, leaving the potential lost beneath a layer of blue ice.

The days grew colder that week, and, while the sky remained still and clear, the air was heavy with the scent of new snow, tickling and teasing, winter's mix of threat and promise. The snow would come soon. Katie hoped Mrs. Tallbear would remember to send someone to fix her roof before the bigger storms came. The leak had grown worse, and would grow worse still with every cold, passing hour and day. When the wind came, it spilled through the leak, giving the house a moaning, sorrowful voice like the sounds of a ghost: a bit of the past trapped like a fish in a frozen lake. Katie thought about calling, but her mobile service on the island sucked. If she wanted to ask about the handyman, she'd probably have to go all the way back to Aurora.

Katie pulled on her coat and mittens and went outside to stare up at the corner where the leak had spread like a crack in a glacier. She should climb up and clear away some of the ice, she decided. She should. That might help, a little bit anyway. Chipping it away would be a start towards fixing things. She chewed her lower lip for a long moment. Perhaps she would do it tomorrow. Or maybe she would go back into town and ask Mrs. Tallbear about the repairman. Or at least try calling. Maybe she'd have good phone karma that day.

She could even tell the woman that she'd started painting again. It was only a little lie. After all, she had started. Sort of. She had put down a base coat, and there was victory in that, even if it hadn't been enough to warm her stilled creativity.

There were other things that needed doing as well, of course. There always are, when one lives alone, especially in the Alaskan winter. But Katie didn't do any of them.

She should bring in more wood for the iron box by the fireplace: she wouldn't want to venture outside when the snows came again. This late in the winter, they would last for days. She didn't venture outside, though, not even to the woodpile just a few paces away. And she'd planned to make a big batch of savory vegetable stew, enough to last for a few days. But to do that, she'd have to wash her large pot. Instead, she nibbled at a carrot and left the rest alone. Her will to life needed some kind of CPR, but she was no self-care paramedic of the soul.

She settled in her bed and picked up a book, but she never turned a page. When she squinted, the tiny black and white words seemed to blur and move, like a city of ants racing hither and yon in a still, quiet world of white and gray. The lethargy had grown comfortable, like a heavy blanket pulled up and wrapped around her shoulders and throat, like a cocoon woven against the cold. She stayed still, still and numb.

Now and again she remembered the man from the pub, the lovely man who'd spoken to her.

"God," she muttered aloud one afternoon, "no man should be allowed to be that beautiful."

The thought brought a warm blush to her cheek, so she forced him from her mind.

Instead, she thought of Billy. If she'd thought of another man, even fleetingly, well, wasn't that a good sign? Was she getting over Billy at last? Was she healing? The pain wasn't there, that terrible, burning pain that had made her leave her Boston loft and run all the way to the end of the world.

Katie sat still and thought about Billy for a long time. He'd had such lovely eyes, and such strong, calloused hands, even though he'd never looked at her when he touched her. He'd always looked away, as if he were ashamed, or embarrassed, or afraid. Or—now she admitted it—like he'd been distracted. Like he hadn't really cared. Maybe all of those things at once. She wasn't sure how she felt about that. She tried to muster something, just to see what would come. Anger at his leaving? Hurt where the wound surely remained open, a gape in the heart? Passion, maybe? Love? Was that still there?

Did she still . . . want him?

She didn't know.

Instead she felt simply . . . nothing. Empty like the blue canvas, without shape or color, silent and still. In the bitter cold of the dark Alaska winter, she was numb.

She didn't get out of bed at all the next day. Not because she was tired, or lazy, or even because she liked the self-indulgent luxury of resting beneath the heavy, fallen drifts of flannel and down. It was simply because she couldn't think of a reason to expend the energy to rise.

The next day her stomach rumbled like the ground in an earthquake. She was hungry, so she climbed out of bed and ate a bowl of cereal. Afterwards, she spent the rest of the day flitting about her tiny house, haunting its rooms like a spirit too insubstantial to disturb even the dust or the patterns of frost on the cold windowpanes.

Katie tried counting snowflakes for a while, but decided that, too, was a waste of time; so instead she counted only the ones that were just alike. The time passed slowly.

The day after was Sunday, the last Sunday of Advent. Katie thought briefly about making an Advent wreath; as a child, she'd done so every year. It was a part of the season, like gifts and carols and *Rudolf* on TV. She didn't bother, though. It didn't seem worth the trouble just to light the one last candle. Besides, she didn't have any holly or tinsel.

She thought about going into town instead. She should check her mail, because there might be Christmas cards. She could set them up on her mantle after she'd read them, and the color would brighten up her drab, gray house. Of course, she'd have to answer them, but maybe that wouldn't be so bad. A little contact with people and her past might be a good thing. Why shouldn't it be? And while she was in town, she could enjoy the gilt and charm of the town's holiday decorations. They were warm and lovely and wonderful, even with all those ravens scattered about like specks of coal. Katie loved Christmas decorations, even if they were too much trouble for just one person alone in a tiny house.

But she didn't go to town.

Maybe she would tomorrow.

Maybe.

When afternoon came, Katie thought about calling home. The sky was clear; maybe she'd have good luck with her phone. Her family would already be at the Cape house for the holiday. She missed her family sometimes. It would be good to hear their voices. When she closed her eyes, she had a hard time remembering what they sounded like. It's a hard thing, a hard and terrible thing, the first Christmas spent alone at the end of the world where everything is cold and white, so far, so far away from home. Without the weight of time and tradition, she felt light. In the end, she didn't call. They would want things from her. They would only plead with her to come back, to come back home, back to life and warmth and the world. At the very least, they would demand promises for future calls. When? *When?* Katie wasn't ready for that, not yet. *Oh God, not yet, not yet.* Nor for the rush of memories the voices would bring, punching and piercing through her comfortable shields like ice picks. She wanted to stay in her cocoon. It's just too hard to remain numb when the Ghost of Christmas Past pesters and rattles you with all that is bright and lost.

In the end, she wandered back to the studio room and forced herself to spend the day staring at her blocks of stone and plaster, hoping that guilt might drive her where inspiration failed. It didn't. Guilt was an anchor; she needed wings. Inspiration was lost, lost like stars are: vanished behind heavy, brooding winter clouds when the dark sky is cold and black, but empty, and even promises are forgotten.

Katie shivered. The studio room was even colder than the rest of the house, especially with the leak in the roof; but Katie stayed there anyway, wrapping her arms across her breasts. The air was heavy with bitter chill and the scent of impending snow grew stronger.

5

A Pot Can Be a Canvas, Can't It?
And Spices Can Be a Palette

 knock at the door startled Katie. She sat bolt upright, knocking her table and upsetting her tea mug. The tea had gone cold. In all the months she had been here, there had never been a knock at the door. It had been so long since she'd heard one that she'd forgotten what they sounded like.

The knock came again. For a second, Katie panicked. What was she supposed to do? What was expected of her? Her heart pounded and her face felt flushed. She looked down; she couldn't remember if she'd dressed that morning. She had. She shook her head. The knock came twice more, sharp raps, before she composed herself enough to leap to her feet and hurry to answer it.

Her pulse quickened as she ran. Her fingers, once nimble but suddenly clumsy, had to fumble with the locks before she could pull the heavy door open. A man stood there, bundled in heavy layers beneath parka, hood, and gloves.

"Hi there," he said, his voice deep and friendly, as he pulled back his fur-lined hood. "Katie, right? Remember me? I'm Lucas Tulukkam. From New Sam's place?"

As soon as he smiled, she knew the face, even though she'd only see it one brief time. But it took her an awkward second to place it, because it was so far out of its context. The man from the pub, the lovely Inuit man, stood gazing at her expectantly.

She wasn't sure what to say, how to react. She simply stood there, stunned, frozen, staring dumbly, mouth and eyes wide open.

"I'm sorry," said Lucas. "I didn't mean to surprise you. I thought you were expecting me?"

Katie didn't know how to answer.

"Guess not."

What was he doing here? Did he know, somehow, did he know she'd been thinking of him? She'd even spoken of him aloud, she realized. Had she summoned him somehow? Would he be angry? Expectant? What was she supposed to say? She shook off her blanket of lethargy to find words. But she wasn't certain how to begin. The blanket was like snow turned to ice; it was slow to move.

"Um, hello," she said after far too long an awkward moment. "I . . . I'm sorry. God! You just caught me by surprise, that's all."

"That's okay." He smiled expectantly.

Katie didn't answer. She didn't move.

"I guess you don't get too much company up here, do you?" he continued after a moment. "I guess you came up for the peace and quiet and all, and here I am just busting right in on you."

Katie shook her head, hoping to clear it. Fragments of thought and awkward sentence fragments scrambled around in her head, floating and drifting just out of reach like specks of white in a snow globe. Desperately, she reached for a few, snatching and linking them together; spitting them out and hoping they were appropriate.

"Um . . . would you like to come in? Please!"

"Thank you."

Katie didn't think to move aside, and the man made no move to step around her.

"Missus Tallbear sent me," Lucas said, still smiling. "The lady from the store? She said you needed to have your roof fixed. Before the snow comes."

Katie blinked.

"Uh, sorry it took so long. Lot of people had jobs that needed doing, and well, there's not as many handy-men around a town the size of Aurora as you might think. But I got here as quick as I could. You, uh, do need your roof fixed, right?"

"Oh," said Katie. "Oh!"

Lucas smiled again. "I take it that's a yes?"

"Yes!"

"Well, I'd better get started right quick, then. Snow's coming fast. Can you smell it?"

Katie couldn't, but she nodded. "I think so. Yes."

Lucas looked back over his shoulder at the sky, where clouds, gray on white, were building. "Yeap, it's coming right quick, isn't it?"

"What do we do?"

"Well, I've got some tools and lumber and stuff in my truck back on the mainland." He quirked his head back towards the dock. "I thought maybe we'd take your boat over and haul 'em back together. I mean, if you have time."

"Of course! Just, uh, let me get my coat and stuff."

It took almost a full hour to bring the boards, insulation, heavy tarpaper, shingles, and tools back to the island. The snow began to fall, light flurries like scouts before the storm.

"I'd better get started right quick," said Lucas. "I can at least get us a temporary patch up there before it gets too hard."

"What can I do?"

"How 'bout starting a pot of coffee?"

"But . . . is that all?"

"That'd be plenty. If it's no trouble, that is. I can work faster alone, I'm thinking. Just to put a quick patch on. And I'd best do it fast before it gets too slick up there, right?"

"You'll be okay up there, won't you?" Katie frowned. "Is it safe? I mean, you won't, like, fall or anything, will you?"

"Oh, don't worry." Lucas he tossed his tools and the roll of tarpaper up. "Heights aren't nothing to me. Besides, it's not too high up. If I slip, I'll just slide and land me right there in this deep snowbank, see? Soft as a plumped-up feather bed. Then you can come out and dust me off. Deal?"

"Deal." Katie tried to return the smile, but quickly looked away. Despite the slaps of cold wind, her face felt suddenly, unexpectedly warm. "I'll just go start that coffee."

Inside, Katie heard the banging of the hammer as she puttered around in her kitchen. Lucas must be putting on a temporary cover of board and tarpaper, she guessed. That would be enough to last through the storm. They could do something more permanent when it passed, she and Lucas. If he were willing to come back out, anyway. Surely he would be. Wouldn't he? Of course he would. He was a handyman. That was what handymen did. She could pay him. The hammer found a rhythm and Katie danced to the steady cadence— step, filter, spin, water, pirouette, push the button and start the brewing. Soon the scent of fresh coffee filled her cabin. She tried to remember the last time she'd made a whole pot, instead of settling for the instant stuff. She couldn't.

The wind howled more fiercely, and the snow fell in earnest. Katie glanced out of her small kitchen window, the one that looked east. Already, the mainland was lost behind a curtain of swirling white.

I should make something hot, she thought. Food, not just coffee.

But the cans she would have opened and mixed quickly together if she were cooking only for herself didn't seem like enough, somehow. Not nearly, not for company. She supposed Lucas counted as company, even though he'd come on a professional errand. Sure he did. No, no. She needed more than the usual, more than the Spaghetti-Os she would have made for Billy. It had to be more.

Something substantial.

Katie did a quick inventory, starting with the stuff in the freezer she'd barely touched. Ground beef—frozen but available. Canned vegetables, and a few fresh ones, too. Whole bulbs of garlic. A few more assorted herbs and spices: savory, marjoram, basil, sage, thyme, oregano, black pepper. Now where had those come from? Mrs. Tallbear must have given them to her; she didn't remember picking them out. Or maybe she'd picked them up without noticing; she hadn't paid attention, really. Maybe they were a part of someone else's order. Had there been anyone else in the store when she checked out? She couldn't remember. She'd been too busy trying to be insubstantial to notice other people. Besides, it didn't matter; they were here now. But what could she do with them? Did she even have any recipes? Her hands were accustomed to shaping stone, not preparing meals. That was totally different.

Or was it?

Dammit, you're an artist, she told herself. A pot can be a canvas, can't it? And spices can be a palette. Well, why the hell not?

She sliced and chopped, dashed and spooned, tasted and mixed. Then she combined it all, wielding her mixing spoon like a paintbrush, alternating between strokes bold and subtle. She started the mixture to boil with the vegetables, then she cooked the meat, scraping off the brown parts as it thawed and seasoning it with pepper and chopped garlic. She even heated a loaf of crusty bread to go with it.

When Lucas came in, shivering from the storm, her small house was warm and filled with steam and the pungent scents of simmering stew and freshly brewed coffee. The fierce, icy wind shook and tore through the house, rattling the walls and making the fire flicker and roar before Lucas managed to shove the door closed again. Katie shivered in the unexpected cruelty of the sudden chill before the besieged warmth could reestablish itself.

"Hey," said Katie. "Jesus, look at you. You're just about all frozen to death!"

Lucas smiled, that lovely, dazzling smile of his, and Katie felt light: like a cloud, like wind. He shook himself, sending a flurry of white drifting down to melt on the mat by the door.

"I'll be just fine," he promised. "See? I got your roof all patched right up. Good enough for the storm, anyway. Now I just need to thaw out a little. How's that coffee coming along?"

"It's ready," said Katie. "See? And there's some warm food, too. Or there will be, soon. It's stew, so it needs to simmer a bit."

She handed him a mug. "Here, in the meantime. Want anything in it?"

"I'll just take it black, thanks." He smiled and raised it to her in salute. Katie smiled and raised her own mug. They drank their coffee together, and Lucas told her more about the condition of her roof, and what more would have to be done both in the short and long run. Later, Katie couldn't remember a single thing he said, except that she'd loved the sound of his voice, and since he was the one with all the information, he'd had to do most of the talking, so she could remember the subtleties of conversation slowly, like exercising muscles stiff from disuse.

When he'd finished, Katie remembered the stew, and hoped it had simmered long enough. She was glad she'd used ground beef rather than stew beef that would have had to tenderize.

"Come on," she said. "Sit down! I'll make you a bowl."

Grinning, Lucas obeyed. "Can I have some more of that coffee, too?"

The coffee was good. To Katie's surprise and delight, the stew was even better. It was bright and unusual, original and bold, like a picture painted by a folk artist with vision and great talent but no training.

As they ate, the snow grew worse, far worse than either of them had expected.

After the meal, they sat together on Katie's small sofa, and she continued to rediscover the art of casual conversation and the joys of learning about another person. Lucas was quick-witted and mercurial, and if he didn't reveal too much about himself, well, that was okay. He didn't ask many questions, either. He didn't expect anything of her, not finished art nor explanations about her breakup with Billy. He smiled and laughed and enjoyed. That was enough.

She wondered, more out of habit than any real concern. If she should be nervous about having a near stranger in her house, especially when she was so far from any neighbor. As soon as the thought occurred to her, she let it go, rather to her surprise. Something about Lucas made her comfortable. Besides, Mrs. Tallbear had sent him, so she trusted him. New Sam knew him, too. Katie relaxed and let herself enjoy.

Night came, but the storm never let up. It was too dangerous to travel, so, in the deepest part of the cold winter night, Katie invited Lucas to stay.

"The snow's not going to let up, you know. It's too dangerous to drive. I'm not even sure I can get you back to your truck. My boat—"

"Now I don't want to be any trouble," Lucas said, smiling again and holding up his hands.

Katie couldn't look at him.

"It's no trouble at all," she said softly. I can get some blankets—"

"And it's not like I'm exactly a stranger to snow. Besides, I knew it was coming when I drove up here. So it's my own fault."

"Just to fix my stupid old roof. You shouldn't have."

He shrugged. "I couldn't leave it leaking, not with the storm coming. Maggie Tallbear would have my hide! She'd tack it up on her wall or lay it down on the floor like a rug. You wouldn't want me stretched out on some cold floor, would you?"

"I don't want you stretched out by some road, either. Please stay. It's too icy to drive."

"Well, okay then. If you're sure it's not going to be any kind of trouble."

"No trouble," Katie promised. "Besides, I can't eat all that stew by myself." So *substantial. . . .*

She made him a bed on the sofa, tucking herbs, lavender, and dried flower petals under the corners of the blankets to make him sleep soundly and dream lovely dreams. He smiled when she bid him goodnight and slipped into the shadows in her own bedroom.

"Good night, Katie!" he called after her. She, too, dreamed lovely dreams that night, dreams of Christmas and winter, of clouds and golden sky.

In the morning, Katie climbed out of bed and pulled on a terrycloth robe over her flannel nightshirt. She stepped into bedroom shoes over the socks she slept in, both to keep her feet warm and to hush her steps. She found Lucas still asleep, so she started a pot of fresh coffee and went back to her room to dress quietly.

She watched her guest sleep for a moment, and marveled that his dark and angular features could be so lovely even when still. Awake, they were always in motion. She liked how his hair had rumpled on the pillow. Then, suddenly shy—and worried that he might wake and catch her staring—she pulled on her coat and mittens and stepped out onto her back porch.

Dawn had come, shining golden dimness across a still landscape of stark and brilliant white. The cold was sudden and astonishing; it rattled her bones and chilled her blood with a swiftness that startled her. Across the narrow water that separated her little island from the mainland, she could see a gentle swell where the evening's snow had buried Lucas' truck.

The sky was clear, but the clouds on the horizon were black. She wasn't sure if they were coming or going, the augur of a new storm or the memory of the last one, but they looked ominous all the same.

He probably won't be able to leave today, she realized. He'll have to stay a while.

She smiled as she came back inside. Lucas was just starting to stir.

"Hiya," he said, his voice still heavy with sleep. "Good morning!"

"Morning. Want some coffee?"

"Umm," he said, nodding. "Smells mighty good. And a shower, too, if you don't mind too much."

"Go ahead. There's a clean towel by the sink. I'm afraid all the shampoo is girlie."

Lucas chuckled drowsily. "I'll make do."

"Go ahead, then. I'll see if I can find us some food."

After a breakfast of bacon, eggs, and buttery cinnamon toast, Lucas climbed back onto the roof to check his patch. It seemed to be holding, he reported. But the scent of coming snow was still in the air, even though most of the sky was clear. Katie's nose twitched, and she frowned.

"Ah, you smell it too, eh? Yeah. It's going to snow again. Soon."

Katie squinted, looking for a sign of moving cloud. Were they coming or going? "You sure?"

He nodded. "Hour, maybe. Two at most. Not enough time for a proper repair. Not if we want to do it all good and right. And that's the only way to do things if you ask me."

"Well, come on back in, then. No reason it can't wait, is there? I mean, you got it patched and all."

"No reason at all," Lucas agreed with a smile. The snow came again an hour and a half later.

Katie found three games up on the shelf in her closet, Scrabble, Monopoly, and a chess set. They played Scrabble and Monopoly until lunchtime, and then, since neither knew how to play chess, they used the board and pieces for checkers. After that, they made up story games using the chess pieces as characters.

"My knight chases off the mean old pointy-head guy," said Lucas, grinning slyly.

"Oh ho!" cried Katie. "But my king steps in—" she moved the piece a few spaces—"and blocks your wicked advance, rogue!"

Lucas tipped the black knight over. "Then my bold knight dies of a broken heart. But look! Here comes *my* king!"

"Oh! I flee!" Katie pushed her queen back to the end of the board, behind her row of pawns. Then she lifted the back of her hand to her forehead, feigning a swoon.

Lucas's king pursued Katie's queen, and when he caught her at last, he presented her with his two castles and all his pawns, telling her they were tiny spirits who could grant wishes. Katie laughed so hard that her side and jaw ached, and she had to blow her nose.

They spent the rest of the day talking and laughing. When the sun dipped down behind the mainland, she warmed more of the stew and they ate it together.

After dinner, Katie told Lucas about Boston, with its narrow, winding streets and tiny pubs. She told him about Italian restaurants in North End. "Did you know that every block in the North End has at least three or four Italian restaurants? Each cozier and more delicious than the last, and that's not even counting, like, the bakeries and cheese shops. Did you know?"

"I didn't even know there was a place called the North End," said Lucas. "Tell me some more."

Katie did. She told him about sailboats in the harbor, and brass ducklings in the Common. She told him about her tiny apartment, just a few blocks from the Wonderland station, at the very end of the MTA Blue Line.

Lucas, in turn, told Katie about Alaska and about sea and hill and snow and sky. He claimed to know a polar bear, and the story made Katie laugh again. It was a strange feeling, that laughter, like trying to do a cartwheel when you haven't done one since you were a girl.

"Tell me some more," Katie said. "Tell me about Aurora."

"What about it?" asked Lucas.

"I told you all about Boston—"

"Not *all*," Lucas pointed out.

"Tell me about Aurora. Tell me a story."

"There's a story about Raven," said Lucas.

"And Aurora?"

"And *the* aurora," said Lucas. "The aurora borealis. The northern lights. Do you know about Raven?"

Katie nodded. "Mrs. Tallbear told me about him, about how he stole all the light from the selfish chief, and how he wakes the world."

Lucas nodded. "Well, then you know how old Raven, he likes shiny things. Well, one day he's off flying around, looking for new skies to explore, and it happens that he flies up north, out where everything is still and white, and where the ice never melts, not even in summer."

"Up here?"

"Oh, even further up than here, I expect. Anyway, Raven looks up, and aren't the stars just as bright as anything, brighter than all the jewels in all the world. Sort of like tonight, I reckon. Why, he's never seen anything so bright, not even when he saw them up close, when he stole them from the selfish chief so they could light the world. But then, sure enough, didn't that old trickster see something else, something just as bright, or maybe even a little brighter? And right there in the sky, too!"

"The aurora?"

"The aurora, sure enough. Now old Raven, he likes shiny things, so you can bet he wanted that pretty light all

John Adcox

for his own. Maybe he thought he could use it to line his nest like a blanket, like a blanket of light. I don't know, and the story doesn't say. All I know is that Raven wanted that light, for his very own, mind, and so off he flew.

"He flew and he flew, Raven did, and he flew farther than he'd ever flown before, farther than he even knew there was to fly. And then he kept right on flying some more, ever north, after that bright curtain of dancing light. Eventually now, eventually he came right to the very edge of the world. There was a great abyss there, a deep, dark place that no one had ever crossed before. No one alive, anyway, because that was the land of the great spirits, the first Mysteries. That old abyss didn't stop old Raven, because he is one of the first Mysteries, too, even though he doesn't always remember it.

"And sure enough, he found the aurora borealis itself, shining just as pretty as you please. And when he found it, he found that it was more than light. It was music, too, music like the stars make. And old Raven was about to roll up that light right up and take it back to his nest, but just then, he realized what it was. It was an echo, an echo of the very first light, that first shine called forth by the first Maker with the very first music, the very first world, at the very beginning of all the words and worlds. The first Maker had left it there so that all the people could see it, and so we'd all know we hadn't been forgotten, and that we were never alone, and that we were loved. Always, forever. That was a sacred thing, even to ol' Raven.

"Now Raven, he might have rolled that light up anyway, but just then, why, something shiny caught his eye, a pearl, white as the sea foam, bright as the first snow. It was a way to the south, shining like the moon. So away he went, flying south, looking for that pearl. And so the aurora borealis still shines in the northern sky, even today, and we can all look up and remember."

"Did he find it?" Katie asked.

"Find what?"

"The pearl."

"I expect he did," said Lucas. "He probably tricked somebody out of it and took it right back to his nest. But I don't know for sure. The story doesn't say."

"Mmmm," said Katie. "I like that."

Lucas smiled. "I'd hoped you might."

"But I wanted to hear about this Aurora, the town." *I wanted to hear about your home. I wanted to hear about you.* He hadn't told her anything about himself, not really. But that was only fair. She hadn't really told him anything, either.

"Next time."

"Next time," Katie agreed, and she wondered if he hadn't meant it, either.

Night came, and Katie made Lucas's bed for him again. Impulsively, she gave her guest a fast hug, then turned and fled to the darkness of her own room.

"Good night, Katie!" he called after her.

71

"Good night, Lucas," she said softly. She was sure he'd heard her.

She felt the warmth of his touch lingering through the night. It snowed again as they slept.

6

Cold and Pungent Intensity

n the third day, Katie and Lucas became lovers.

In the morning, they made breakfast. They created omelets, each of them taking turns adding dashes of this odd favorite, or splashes of that unexpected spice, something remembered, dimly, faded like a photograph left too long in the sun, from favorite breakfasts made long ago. The result was a sagey, sausagey hodgepodge, a potion conjured from old and new, from almost forgotten to newly discovered, like art created from experience of the past and thrill of vision, from memory and dream. Katie wasn't used to collaborating; she was only a little surprised to find that she liked it.

For a moment, Katie wondered if the sudden interest in cooking might be a hint of the artist in her reemerging. She didn't like where that thought seemed to lead, so she pushed it away, unthought, quickly and thoroughly, to a cold and dark closet in the back of her mind and locked the door firmly behind it.

They ate together at Katie's little table. The first bites were too shocking to be pleasant, sweet and bitter and salty all at the same time, but by the time she finished she'd decided she liked it.

At that moment, she caught Lucas gazing at her, and she recognized something she hadn't seen since in a long time, not since Billy used to look at her that way, before the final silence fell between them like a curtain, empty, cold, and absolute.

She found herself wishing she could save some of the breakfast, hidden away like a snowball saved in the freezer for golden July, so that she could preserve the flavors for some summer day, slow and sultry, when winter was a memory and the moment, with all its cold and pungent intensity, was faded and lost. Then she would feel Lucas's eyes upon her again, even as her own gaze grew bold and wise in the pale morning light. She would look away then, too, because she knew her eyes, shining and deep, held secrets that women hold close and men were never meant to know. She would show him a hint, quick but penetrating, before she turned her attention back to her steaming coffee mug; and then, she knew, he would carry that glance with him, teasing like the brush of a snowflake against his cheek, for the rest of the day.

After breakfast, Lucas went outside to clear away the snow from the roof and start working on the repair. Katie, suddenly and acutely alone, went to her studio and stood in the doorway, looking in. She didn't enter; she was afraid that if she did, an intensity would reawaken, and the forms hidden in the solid blocks would call her and beg to be freed with silent voices too urgent to be ignored. She wasn't ready for art, no, not yet.

The draft made it cold in the doorway, but she found that from there, she had a vantage point: near but not too close, neither in nor out but merely between. There she could look on and feel the call, faint like the sound the waves make as they freeze or thaw, and not be overwhelmed by the agony of inspiration. For a moment, just a moment, she almost went in. She'd nearly forgotten what it was like, to see with her artist's eye through the depth of possibility to the truth caught within.

But no, no. *God no.*

It wasn't time for creation, no, not yet.

The moment passed. While Lucas worked above, she spent the day in the doorway, watching the shapes in the stones, dim and distant, moving like the shadows of fishes swimming slowly beneath the frozen surface of a winter lake.

The wind howled with new ferocity, and Lucas came down and in for a break. "It's worse than I thought," he admitted, "but nothing I can't handle. Don't you worry."

While he rested and waited for the sky to calm, they played games again, this time using the chess pieces with the Monopoly set. You could buy properties and build houses, or you could try to take them with king and pawn. Queen or bishop could gain monopolies by demanding that the other player answer riddles (that was Lucas's idea, but Katie was better at it). Castles could replace hotels, and command twice the rent, but the pawns could lay siege, and that presented just all kinds of problems because black pawns and white pawns had different powers, and because the rules changed depending on whether the attack began on an even minute or an odd one, or if the pawns came via railroad.

"We should have given the castles basements," Lucas suggested. "So they couldn't move around so much."

Katie sighed with a great deal of drama. "What good is a castle if you can't move it around when you need to?"

"There's lots of castles in the world. Most of them don't move, do they? They're plenty good, or so it seems to me."

"These," Katie insisted, "are better."

Lucas went back to the roof. When he came back inside at last, shivering and making a small blizzard with the snow he shook off his coat, Katie made warm cider with cloves, lemon, honey, and cinnamon sticks. She sat with him on her worn, old sofa and listened as he told stories of the places he'd seen and all his travels across lands where the natives have a thousand words for snow and none for cold, because they know of nothing with which to contrast it. For them, cold is synonymous with existence. The stories were lovely; they made Katie smile and laugh. But they weren't the ones she wanted to hear. They still weren't about him, not really. But hers, again, weren't really about her, either. She'd never even mentioned Billy. Maybe that was for the best. As a child raised on fairy tales, Katie knew that the wrong question can break a spell.

When the talking stopped, they simply sat together and listened to what the silence would reveal. After a time, Katie dozed. When she woke, her head was resting on Lucas's shoulder and his arm stretched around her, keeping her warm. Deep in her heart, she knew that if she moved, Lucas would smile and joke, and the moment, with its comfortable, casual intimacy, would melt away in a springtime of laughter and activity. So instead she closed her eyes and let herself sleep again, dozing safe in the harbor of his arms. She dreamed of flight and shiny treasure.

Later, she opened her eyes to find that Lucas had drifted off to sleep. Slowly and gently, she disentangled herself from his arms, careful not to wake him. She took the last of the stew and placed it on the stove, ready to heat, in case Lucas was hungry when he roused himself. It would be close to suppertime, she guessed. Since neither of them had eaten lunch, it was probably close enough to suppertime already. She put a bottle of good red wine just inside the door, where fingernails of Arctic wind reached in to chill it. She liked it cool, but not cold like it would be if she put it in the refrigerator. Room temperature, but the coolest part of the room. She hoped Lucas would like it that way, too.

She wandered back into the main room and watched Lucas sleep for a few moments.

Oh God, she thought. *He's even more beautiful when he's asleep!*

Katie's face grew warm, so she turned and fled until she felt her cheeks grow cool and pale once again and the unexpected passion was numbed. She found herself in the studio doorway once again, and for a long moment the desire to make came upon her like a fever, burning, so desperate in its intensity that her whole body shook like a madman's in a fit of sudden and astonishing religious ecstasy. Beads of sweat moistened her forehead, glowing like sparkles of water in the sun.

And then she was aware, suddenly, of another doorway, one inside her, shifting like snow in the wind. She felt the doorway to the cold and frozen attic in her brain where she'd locked away her creativity come open, just a notch, and she felt lost things stir.

Katie panicked.

Because in that moment, she knew that there was more than unborn art behind that doorway in her mind. There was fire there, and pain.

Fire. *Pain.*

In her mind's eye, Katie saw herself throw her body against that door, slamming it shut. If avoiding that burning, terrible fire meant she'd never create again, so be it. She could live with that. Let the shapes remain unmade, caught and frozen. She would continue; she would exist.

She held the door in her mind closed, the fire locked and buried away, and she felt herself grow safely cold and numb again. Her heart was pounding. She breathed deeply, slowly, in and out, until it slowed.

She stayed there, in the doorway, neither in nor out of her studio, until at last Lucas came and joined her. Without speaking, he stood behind her and put his arms around her waist, pulling her close, so that her back pressed lightly against his chest, and the top of her head rested beneath his chin. Her body tensed for a moment, and then she relaxed. They stood that way, together, for a long time, and Katie found herself surprised by the comfort and quiet pleasure of the casual contact. Billy had never held her like this. For him, touch was always a prelude to sex, never for the joy of simple closeness. Katie liked it. She sighed and snuggled closer into Lucas's embrace.

After a time, minutes or hours, Lucas spoke. "Is this your work?"

He was looking past her, into the studio.

"It's supposed to be," Katie admitted.

"I like that one." Lucas was looking at the block of granite from which Katie had freed the single, grasping arm before she'd abandoned the piece. "I see a man crouching, like he's under a lot of pressure, or pressed down by some way heavy weight. Is that right?"

Katie nodded, unable to speak.

"And he's reaching up, isn't he? Like he's reaching to Heaven, you know? To, like, God or something. You know?"

Katie's heart skipped a beat.

No one, no one had ever been able to see the shapes caught in stone, ghosts, shadows of possibility, not before she'd freed them with skill and strength of arm. But Lucas, Lucas seemed to see, yes, to *know!*

How could it be? Was he looking at the granite the same way she did? Or was he, somehow, seeing inside her? She wanted to ask him about it. Her mouth opened, but the words weren't there. Her heart pounded and her eyes opened wide.

Lucas frowned. "But I can't quite read his expression. It's like . . . it's like the face is hidden. You know? Is he desperate, or is that ecstasy in his eyes?" Katie felt him shake his head. "Is it joy or despair? Longing or communion?"

"I . . . I don't think I even know."

She'd never been able to see the face, either. Now that her art was no longer about Billy, she wasn't sure what the stone hid, or what truth burning with painful intensity would be revealed when she found and shaped the face at last. She'd been afraid to look.

"I guess I'll find out when I get to it. If I ever do."

"What's stopping you?"

Katie shrugged, knowing Lucas would feel the slight motion even if he couldn't see it. "I don't know."

"You can tell me," said Lucas, and he held her more tightly. Katie could feel the warmth of his breath against the back of her neck. His arms were strong across her belly. "What is it?"

"I don't know what to say," she whispered. She was glad that Lucas still held her, so that she didn't have to look into his face and meet his gaze.

"Isn't that why you came all the way up here?" Lucas asked her. "To make art? That's what Missus Tallbear told me, anyway. Back at the store."

Katie nodded. "And to heal."

"I see," said Lucas. "So you've been hurt."

It wasn't a question, but Katie nodded again.

"And let me guess. You're thinking that before you can do all that healing, you've got to face it all somehow. All the hurt. And you need to do that before you can make art again. That's it, isn't it?"

Fire and pain. To get to the place where art was born, she'd have to walk through that terrible, burning fire. Her soul's skin would blister, blacken and crack, and her spirit's blood would boil to ash. Before she could create again, she was going to hurt. A part of her had always known that, she realized. That's why she'd fled to a safe, frozen place, a place where she was numb. Cold made her safe.

"I think so," said Katie.

"Well. I see. I reckon."

"I guess I'm just, like, just all kinds of major screwy, huh?"

"Oh, hardly," Lucas said. "'Course, I'm no kind of expert." Katie could hear the grin in his voice, and she laughed. "Sounds to me like you just need to rest for a while. Like the world in winter. Don't you think?"

"Maybe so."

"Or maybe . . . I don't know. Maybe I can help you."

No! Katie swallowed. "I don't think so," she said. *Oh God no!* "I mean, not yet. Okay?"

"Why not?"

"I . . . I don't know."

"Is it 'cause you're not ready?"

"Not yet," Katie repeated. "Maybe in the spring. That's soon enough, don't you think?"

"I guess so."

"Because right now, I just want to be cold." *And numb.*

"Why's that?"

"Because . . . Oh, God!" She started to cry.

"You can tell me, Katie. Really."

Because the door in her mind was made of ice, and it was starting to melt.

"Because it's going to *hurt*," Katie said. And then she was crying in earnest.

"Oh, Katie, I'm so sorry! Really, I was just trying to help!"

Carefully and gently, Lucas turned her around, so that her face was against his chest, and held her close. Katie sobbed.

"Don't worry, Katie, please don't worry. You just keep right on resting as long as you need to. I don't want you to hurt, honey. Listen to me. Okay? You just stay cold. I mean, if that's what you want. I'll protect you."

Lucas kept talking. His voice was gentle and soothing, like a caress, like snow, or like rose scented bubbles in a warm bath. She let them pour over her, pulling them close around her like threads in a white cocoon.

"You don't have to hurt in spring, Katie. You can stay cold as long as you want, dear heart, really. I promise. Don't worry about spring, or warmth, or hurt, or art and old stone. No. Don't worry about anything. Winter will keep us safe and still. We'll bury ourselves in snow, like children in an icy womb. Won't we? Sure we will. The snow's a blanket, don't you see? Why, it'll keep us safe, you just see, and it'll freeze away all the hurt and danger. I'll protect you, Katie. I'll keep you safe, okay?"

Katie cried until no more tears were left inside her. And when at last her body stopped trembling, she lifted her face to his and kissed him, drinking him down like old whiskey.

That night she slept with her naked body pressed against Lucas's, skin against skin. Katie dreamed of an explosion of lilies and spring flowers blooming like bursting popcorn kernels, and for some reason of peculiar dream logic, the explosion of color unnerved her, bringing her close to shuddering panic. But when Lucas touched and kissed them, the blossoms turned to snowflakes, crystalline and delicate, and she slept through the winter, smiling, safe beneath a heavy blanket of purest white.

In the morning, she awoke in Lucas's arms. They'd slept all night with the shades open, so the cold morning light left a pale, luminous grid across the white sheets and a crisscross of dark stripes across their still entwined bodies. For a long time, Katie watched Lucas sleep, tracing the chilly play of light and shadow moving across his skin. When he woke, he smiled at her. They spent the day learning as much about each other as sound, sight, touch, and taste could teach. They ate, they slept, they laughed, they made love. Snow came again, but the roof held.

"I need to fix that more permanently," Lucas said.

"After the snow," said Katie. Stay, she thought. "There's plenty of time."

Lucas stayed.

Katie and Lucas didn't decorate for the holidays. "You sure you don't want to?" Lucas asked her one morning.

"I don't," said Katie. For some reason she couldn't begin to articulate, she didn't want to celebrate Christmas, or New Year's either, because marking even the holiest or most significant of days was to acknowledge the passage of time as it shifted its great weight and pulled them along, helpless, like flotsam caught in the gray-green and crashing waves of a stormy December sea. The time she spent with Lucas was like an everlasting day preserved in a snow globe of the heart, safe and unchanging. Katie was afraid that if she looked, if she acknowledged the motion of calendar or clockwork, the spell would vanish like frost on a chimney stone.

Instead, they let the days pass slowly, drifting one after another, snowflakes in a gentle storm, in a kind of calm and changeless bliss. Snow covered the world, and Katie's numbness was replaced with a different stillness, still like sleep, a kind of quiet and comfortable winter joy.

7

An Adam and Eve of a Winter Eden

anuary gave way to February, February to March, and March to April. Katie scarcely knew the passage of days and months. She began to think of her little house on its lonely island as a cottage in that snow globe. Outside, the days flashed by, one fading into another, like cars racing by on a freeway. Snows fell, leaving her small world isolated and unchanged, protected in its womb of frosted crystal.

Katie and Lucas spent the days together, learning the secrets and idiosyncrasies only lovers know. Once when they made love, Katie felt his warmth in the depths of her, a root in the womb of the earth, and in that instant, the world was bright and golden, and she felt as though she were seeing it all, the two of them, the narrow bed, the cabin, the island, and the ice-frosted land, from above, high and soaring. In that moment, she wanted desperately to join with Lucas, not to be connected, but to be one, flying, light, the way moth and candle are one for a single agonizing moment of shining, blazing, golden bliss.

Afterwards, she wept softly, her body trembling, and Lucas held her. He whispered gently in her ear, words like soft kisses, until she was still. They dozed together until morning turned to afternoon, and a new blanket of snow covered the tiny house on its island.

They laughed and talked together; they invented new games and told stories. When the road was safer, Lucas went to town—he had jobs to do and, as he had pointed out, there's not as many handymen around a town the size of Aurora as you might think. When he came back late that night, he brought a truckload of groceries—wonderful surprises, like strange fruits from sun-kissed southern places, applewood smoked bacon, mushrooms, salmon, cakes, ales, wines, and breads—that Katie wouldn't have bought for herself. They improvised recipes and cooked wonderful meals, eccentric and hearty.

They gasped and cried together as each came to know the taste and feel of the other's most intimate geography.

The snows came again and kept the rest of the world far away, but Katie and Lucas didn't mind. Their love was a planet all its own and they were its first citizens, an Adam and Eve of a winter Eden.

Lucas loved candles, so every night, Katie lit dozens of them and scattered them throughout the house, turning the rooms into galaxies with tiny golden lights flickering like stars. He laughed and his eyes were bright.

"Shhh," he told her once. "Listen. The candles make music. Can you hear it? It's the sound of their shimmering and warmth."

Katie giggled. "You're silly."

"It's what the universe is made of, that light," said Lucas. "When the first Maker cried 'Light!' at the beginning of all the worlds, it wasn't a shout, no ma'am. It was music, music that called light from the darkness. All the universe is made from that, light and music. Can you hear it?"

"You're silly," Katie said again. But all the same, she quirked her head and listened.

"Shhhh . . . Listen. Listen. Come." Lucas took her in his arms and danced with her. By the time they were finished, Katie thought she *could* hear, almost, a kind of music, like the jingle of bells, soft and distant like stars, the music of flame and moving light.

There were times when Lucas left her. He had work, yes, and there was something wild in him that craved motion and the solitude of open sky and barren landscapes soothed to gentle sloping hills with each new fall of snow.

"Don't go," Katie said sometimes. "Stay with me. Be with me today."

On those sometimes he smiled, and he stayed.

Sometimes, when the call became too strong, he would wander for a day, and sometimes part of a night. Sometimes he took his tools; something he left them behind.

"I'll be back," he would promise her. "Watch for me and light those candles. Okay?" He laughed. "The shining light in the window will call me home!"

Katie would nod, find a smile, and let him go.

When Lucas was gone, Katie found it harder to hush the call of her studio. She would stand in the doorway, looking, looking but never entering, and she could feel the soft blanket of ice swathing her heart begin to stir, to move. She could sense art beneath it, art and the call to make, music like Lucas's first Maker singing light, but she could sense pain, too, buried agony, and terrified, she would flee, flee to food she didn't eat, books she didn't read. And she would wait. And then the blanket around her would still again, like a sheet of ice gentling a winter lake.

Lucas kept his promises. He always returned to her, sometimes with groceries and supplies, sometimes with gifts of smooth stone or bird's feather, and sometimes simply with his smile. And Katie would be there waiting for him, always, surrounded by candlelight like a golden halo, and the bliss of their passion would be reborn in flickering, incandescent light, as though they, the two of them, were the first to touch with desire and need, ever, in the first music when the world was new.

The days remained short and cold, changeless, and the nights long and deep and dark.

Exactly six months after they'd started dating—Katie supposed that was the word—Lucas decided it was high time they had their first date. "Well, why not, huh?" Lucas said. "Why shouldn't I take my best girl into town, and buy her a fancy dinner? Well? I'll even put on my best outfit." He looked down at his boots, black jeans, and gray work shirt. "Which, uh, is pretty much this."

Katie wasn't sure what to say, how to respond. Outside? With people? And food?

"So why not?" Lucas said.

Katie thought she was going to panic, but to her very great surprise, she did not. When Lucas smiled, she found herself smiling back at him. "Why not?"

The town of Aurora, Alaska has exactly five restaurants, assuming you count the two fast food places down by the highway. There is New Sam's pub, of course, a steak place for the tourists, and Mama Gigi's, an Italian place. Lucas took Katie to Mama Gigi's. It was a tiny, narrow space with bare brick walls and exactly twelve tables covered with red and white checkered tablecloths and decorated with candles stuck in wine bottles. Only three of the tables were occupied, but the hostess dutifully asked if they had a reservation. Lucas did.

"Right this way," the hostess said. They followed, and for a moment, Katie felt like all the people there were looking at her, even though there were only a few, and she was pretty sure none of them were. In that moment, Katie felt the old tension rising inside her, trembling, cold, and she wanted to disappear, to float away like a ghost in the mist, to be insubstantial, or to bury herself in deep snow and sleep, lost and forgotten. But when Lucas touched her arm to guide her, she felt herself relax. She smiled, leaning into the touch. She felt altogether connected, like a tree with deep roots, and she found herself trying to remember the last time she'd felt that way. She couldn't.

Lucas held her chair for her. Katie glanced around as she sat and noticed that the framed pictures on the wall were not of Italy, as she'd expected. There were no Colosseums, no Leaning Towers of Pisa, no Venetian canals or gondolas. Her eyes narrowed and she shook her head. "Are those—?"

"Germany," Lucas acknowledged with a nod. "Yep. That's Berlin there, and that one's the German Alps. That's Brandenburg Gate back there. It's famous, you know."

"I do. But . . . in an Italian place?"

"Yep."

"They, uh, know it's not the same thing, right?"

"Oh, we know the difference, sure enough. Even way up here in the last frontier." Lucas winked. "See, Mama Gigi's was opened by a German man who happened to be passing through town. A tourist, I reckon. Before you ask, his name wasn't Gigi, or anything that starts with a G. It was Moritz. This was years ago, but everyone knows the story. Anyway, he fell in love with an Eskimo girl, and next thing he knows, well, he's all married up and putting down roots right here in Aurora. He needed a job, sure, and cooking's what he knew. Of course, as you know, this town's not exactly known for its cuisine, so there weren't many openings for a chef. So he decided to open up his own place. He'd been thinking German, naturally enough, but his new wife thought German was too heavy for the local palate."

"Wow." Katie laughed. "Heavier than spaghetti and pizza? And garlic bread?" *So . . . substantial!* Like an anchor, like roots.

"So it seems. What shall we have?"

Katie laughed again. "Spaghetti and pizza!"

"And garlic bread," said Lucas.

They ordered, they ate, they laughed. Her anxiety was a memory, and soon even that was lost. Talking with Lucas was easy, as natural as breathing. He didn't ask about her past—*Thank God!*—and he didn't insist on telling her about his. They talked about the present, about them, and, suddenly bold, sometimes they talked about the future. Every now and then, their hands touched. When that happened, Katie blushed, not with embarrassment, but with joy. In the gentle light of the candles, everything was golden.

Afterwards, Lucas suggested that they to go to New Sam's place for a drink. "It's Saturday, so they'll have live music," he promised. "Maybe even some dancing."

Much to her surprise, Katie wanted to go, and so they went.

The band played country and classic rock covers, and did so much better than Katie had expected—what they lacked in polish, they made up for in enthusiasm. They changed the lyrics, so every song was not about trucks, or whiskey, or lost love, but about summer, in winter, the heart's fondest desire. Katie laughed so hard that she snorted, and that made them both laugh harder. She had to wipe away a tear.

The crowd was loud and boisterous, and Katie realized that she liked it. She was about to order her usual white wine, but on a sudden impulse she ordered a beer instead. When had she last had a beer? She couldn't remember that, either. Not since before Billy had left. With a start, she realized she hadn't thought about Billy in days, weeks. Not even once. She took a deep sip of her beer and before she could stop herself, she let out a mighty belch. Embarrassed, she covered her mouth with her hand. She blushed and hoped Lucas hadn't noticed. He pretended like he hadn't, and Katie smiled again. *What's happening to me?* Katie wondered. Insubstantial beings didn't snort or belch.

They tried to dance, but it wasn't the right kind of music, not for them, and they fell laughing into each other's arms. Later, they went back to the island and danced to their own secret music.

On a day near the end of May, Lucas brought her a present. He came just as the last light of twilight faded to black and smiled shyly as he handed her a white box tied with a blue ribbon.

Katie untied the ribbon, letting it fall to the floor by the door, and gasped with astonishment. Inside she found a necklace of pearls, each one perfect and glorious blue-white.

"Oh, Lucas," she said as the tears gathered in her eyes. "It's the loveliest thing I've ever seen!"

His smiled widened. "I was so hoping you'd like them."

"Oh Lucas! I love them! But . . . oh dear God! You shouldn't have!"

Lucas raised his eyebrows and tilted his head. "Why ever not?"

"It must have cost a damn fortune!"

"So what's money?" he said with a laugh. His eyes were bright. "It doesn't shine and it isn't lovely at all, not in the least. And look, we have everything we need right here, don't we? I saw a pretty thing, so I brought it home to my sweetheart, where it will be prettier still. Now what's the matter with that?"

Katie smiled and looked down. "Well, nothing, I suppose."

"Besides, it's six months exactly till your birthday, right?"

"How did you know that?"

"Silly. How could I not know when my pretty's birthday is?" She didn't notice that he hadn't answered the question.

"So?"

"Well, up here we celebrate half birthdays, too. The day and the near day."

"The near day?"

"That's the day opposite it on the calendar, exactly six months later. A lot of folks up here think the near day's every bit as important as the day itself, or just about.

"Besides," he added with a wink, "this way it's easier to surprise you! You'da been suspecting something if it was your real birthday, wouldn't you?"

Katie smiled again and hugged him, and promised to put the necklace carefully away, like treasure, until she had an occasion special enough to wear it.

Lucas grinned. "But Katie, every day is special. Isn't it? Don't you think? Especially when we're together."

"Then I'll wear it always."

His smile grew wider, and light twinkled in his dark eyes. He took her in his arms and kissed her, and they both cried with the joy of it. He whirled her, and they danced. Katie's tears splashed on the pearls and sparkled in the light of the candles.

During her times alone, Katie wandered through her small house, loving the way anticipation grew in her like a seed nurtured dark and deep in the garden of the heart. She would prepare ingredients for the evening meal or write notes and scatter them in unexpected places where Lucas was sure to find them. She thought about writing a poem, once, but that was too much like art. When evening came, Katie lit the candles once again, because she knew that their pale and shining glow would guide him home like stars.

Now and then she would still wander past her studio, but even when she happened to go in, the call was silenced. The stones and plaster were only lifeless blocks. Nothing moved. The shapes within were gone, or hidden too deeply to see. Even the shadows of potential form had vanished. Snow covered the room's narrow windows. There was no light; the music was hushed. Katie fingered her string of pearls and chewed her lower lip. The urge to make, and the pain that would surely come with it, was numbed, slumbering like the world in winter.

Katie made a meal, a simple one, one she'd made before, and waited for Lucas to come home. He came, before she'd even finished lighting the candles. They took a walk that night, and Lucas told her stories about the aurora borealis, stories that reminded her, just a little, of Mrs. Tallbear's story about the selfish chief. She wondered if he'd heard them somewhere, or if he'd invented them on the spot. She laughed and clapped her hands. The night was especially cold, and snow was coming, but Katie didn't mind.

Lucas stayed with her the next day, and the day after that. A time or two, Katie heard him on the roof, still working. "Aren't you finished?" she asked.

"It's as good as it was before," he said. "Now I'm making it better. I'da been done with that, too, but . . . you know. Lot of folks have jobs that need doing, right? Anyway. There were a few more patches that'd need repair sooner or later, so why not fix 'em now, while I'm at it? I want my best girl to be safe and snug, no matter what the old weather does. Have to earn my keep, don't I?"

A full week passed before he left again. When he returned, he brought her a present of earrings made from silver and black feathers.

Days passed, and Katie found it easier to pass through the studio door, to actually go into the dark room and walk among the untouched stones and empty canvases, silent like a garden of tombstones. She even cleaned and dusted a little, although she never opened her tubes of paint or disturbed her brushes. The new chisels remained unopened and forgotten on a shelf. There was no call, no music. Her heart remained numb, cold and safe, sleeping like the world in winter, just like Lucas had said.

Long weeks passed before it even occurred to Katie to wonder what had happened to her artist's instincts, the drive that once made her need to make. It was still there, she felt, but it was buried, caught and preserved, lifeless, like the body of some ancient man lost in the blue-white ice of a glacier.

She wondered for a moment if it would return, the terrible drive to sculpt or paint, the hunger, the need, or if the woman she had been was lost forever. She didn't wonder for long. She left the thoughts of art behind her, there with her brushes and chisels. As she left the studio, she noticed that dust had begun to gather again on tools and stone alike. She came back and dusted once more, and then she closed the door behind her when she left.

The days vanished in a wink and the nights were long and cold.

The end of May came before Katie decided to leave the cottage again.

Lucas had gone hiking on the mainland, north, where the stark and beautiful tundra stretched, flat, barren, and changeless, for miles too distant for the mind to comprehend. He promised to return, but he hadn't said when. Katie had seen something of the call in his eyes, though, the wildness, and knew he wouldn't be back that night, and possibly not the next.

Unexpected and intense, a wave of loneliness fell upon her like a shroud. She longed, suddenly, for the world beyond the plain gray walls of her house, and for faces other than her own and Lucas's. She knew that if she waited even a few minutes, it would likely pass, as it always, always did, but for once she decided to indulge it.

Lucas had gone hiking, north, not southeast to town, so he wouldn't return with supplies. Katie studied her cabinets. They were far from bare; she and Lucas wouldn't need anything for a few more days at least.

She shrugged. *What the hell.* She could go just the same. There were at least a couple of people in town who knew her well enough to greet her by name, and several more who knew her face well enough to nod a friendly hello. Maybe she could get another bowl of that chili at New Sam's, without the beans but with the cheddar. Maybe.

She took the boat to the mainland, where her truck was parked next to Lucas's. She cleared off most of the ice and snow, found a classic rock station on the radio, and drove carefully down the icy roads to town.

The Christmas decorations were gone, but aside from that absence, the town looked much the way it had when Katie had met Lucas for the first time, all those cold months before. To Katie, it seemed as though time itself were frozen, like a town in a snow globe. Nothing had changed. Winter had not loosened its grip on Aurora, Alaska; not in the slightest.

Katie parked in front of Mrs. Tallbear's store, but she found it dark and locked up tight. A note on the door explained that Maggie Tallbear was away for a family emergency and instructed anyone in immediate need of supplies to see New Sam at the pub; he had a set of keys.

Katie turned and made her way through the snow to Sam's Old Stonewall Pub.

It wasn't quite lunchtime, but the pub was fairly crowded when Katie stepped in. She didn't mind, though. New Sam grinned and waved to her.

"Hey there," he called. "Katie, right? Long time no see!"

Katie smiled and found a stool at the bar. She studied the menu on the chalkboard while New Sam brought a round of brew to the others at the bar. The menu hadn't changed, but apparently, today's chili wasn't ready, with or without the beans, and yesterday's was gone. When New Sam turned his attention back to her, she ordered a cup of fish chowder and a grilled cheese sandwich. Oh, but she was hungry! Lucas had reminded her what it meant to be hungry.

She was nearly finished when a man came in and took the stool next to her. He was tall, but his hair was silver and his round, Native American features were lined with age. He carried a pipe, but he didn't light it. He ordered coffee and a grilled cheese sandwich with bacon. New Sam promised to hurry it along and disappeared into the kitchen.

The man turned to Katie. "I've seen you before, haven't I? Around town, right?"

Katie knew the face. Maggie Tallbear had pointed the man out when she'd first arrived. He did odd jobs here and there, and guided tourists on wilderness hikes during the season. She nodded.

"A time or two, I think," she said.

"Um," the man agreed. He turned away. "Thought so."

Katie tried to smile. "You sound disappointed."

New Sam returned just then and handed the man a steaming mug of coffee. "Don't mind old Jamie here," he said. "He was hoping you were a tourist."

"Sorry," she said.

"S'okay," the man called Jamie said with a little shrug.

"Lot of folks 'round hereabouts have been waiting for the big boats to come back and bring the tourists," New Sam explained. "When the tourists come, there's work and money."

"I see. When's the season start?"

"Spring," the old man said with a short, bitter laugh. "Which seems to mean never, I reckon."

"So when does spring usually come up here?" Katie asked, her brow furrowing. "Sorry, I haven't been around too long."

"Should have seen some peeps long before now," said New Sam. He shrugged and smiled a crooked little smile. "Never seen anything like this winter, now. Should be warming up at least a little. The ice should be breaking, yeah, and the days should be getting longer."

"Ice should'a done broke," Jamie said without looking up from his sandwich. He brushed a lock of his long, gray hair away from his face. "It's goddamn May! Hasn't happened, though. Ain't *nobody* seen nothing like *this* winter."

"Want anything else, Katie?" New Sam asked. "Some pie, maybe? Or a nice cup of coffee?"

"What kind of pie?"

"Chocolate chess today," New Sam replied. "It's a Southern dish, if you can believe it, and all the way up here in Alaska. Sweet as a kiss and rich enough to make a miser swoon. And the coffee's good and fresh. Want some?"

"Please," said Katie.

"How 'bout you, Jamie?" New Sam asked. "Pie?"

"How 'bout a spot of whiskey to sweeten this coffee a little?"

"Irish?"

"Of course!" The old man sounded offended by the question.

While New Sam scurried off back to the kitchen, Katie found herself frowning. She turned back to Jamie.

"Hey, what did you mean?"

"'Bout the whiskey?"

"About the days not getting any longer?"

"Just what I said," the old man grumbled. "Sun don't come up any earlier, nor stay up any later. And it don't get no warmer, does it?"

Katie felt her brow crinkle. "How can that be?"

Jamie shrugged. "Who can explain it? Should be impossible, eh? It's like winter just don't want to let go none. He's got his claws dug in deep, sure, and the land's frozen all the way down to the root, to the very heart."

Maybe that's not so bad, Katie thought. She'd promised Lucas—and herself—that she'd start making again in the spring. She'd open those doors in the attics of her brain, and she'd face the agony and the loss and all the broken places that waited for her there, that had been waiting ever since Billy left her. She'd thaw, and she'd begin the long, painful process of healing so that she could create again.

But, oh, first she was going to hurt. God, she was going to hurt, with an agony that defied imagination. She shuddered. That could wait. And if spring didn't come, well, that was just fine with her. She could stay snug and still in the comfortable pattern her life had become, protected and secure. Let her artist's heart sleep, frozen in its icy cocoon. In winter, she was numb and safe, just like Lucas had promised.

The tourists will be here soon enough, Katie decided. *Spring can just bloody well wait.*

"The world's still asleep," New Sam said with a hint of a smile as he brought Katie's coffee and refilled Jamie's still steaming mug. He brought the whiskey in a shot glass. "Looks like old Raven has forgotten all about us. You need cream and sugar with that?"

"Please," said Katie. "Raven, huh? Mrs. Tallbear told me about him."

"Did she so?" said New Sam. "She tells a pretty good story, that one."

"Bah," said Jamie. "She's an amateur. Her daddy, now, he could spin you a yarn and that's a fact." Jamie hooked a thumb in his suspenders. "Old Man Twelvetrees, yeah, he's the man who taught me, you know."

New Sam chuckled. "Aren't you supposed to save all that crap for the tourists?"

Jamie chuckled. "Just stayin' in practice, my boy. No tourists comin' this week, I'm thinking."

"Thanks," Katie said wryly.

"So who're you?" asked Jamie. He didn't look up from his coffee. He poured the whiskey in and stirred.

"I'm Katie Mason."

Jamie nodded. "Ah. And what do you do, Katie Mason?"

The name wasn't enough for him. He wanted to know who she was, and for most people, what they did was who they were. For a moment, Katie panicked as she realized she had no idea how to answer him. Before, when she was still with Billy, she'd always had an answer. *I'm Billy Parker's girlfriend,* she could have said. Or, if that wouldn't do, she could say, *I'm an artist. I'm a sculptor; I'm a painter.* But Billy had left; he'd run away to San Diego. He was no longer a part of her identity, of the way she defined herself. And she hadn't made anything in months. Not since long before she'd fled to this stark and white land of sleep and endless winter. That part of her, the maker, was locked away and frozen. Was it still a part of her, of who she was?

Why was it so hard, so hard to be among people? Why did they always seem to expect so much from her? Couldn't they see that she was far, far too numb to have answers?

Who was she? Lucas's lover? His candle-lighter? No, that didn't seem like much of an answer. She had to find Katie before she could let someone, anyone, else be a part of her. Besides, she couldn't even say for sure that she loved him. To love was to commit every fiber of her being to making a relationship work and thrive and grow, nurturing it with all that she was. It was like making art. Katie didn't know how to love halfway. It wasn't in her. To love was to risk all, everything, even to risk being hurt again.

She wasn't ready for that.

Too much of her was numb; too much of her heart was frozen. Making something was lost to her. Even love.

So what, then? Who was she? She found she had no answer.

"I guess I'll do something in the spring," she said at last.

Jamie gave another short, cold laugh.

"Amen," he muttered. He sipped his coffee and motioned for another whiskey. "Won't we all, sure enough, won't we all."

As she drove back toward the dock near her little island, Katie thought about the questions she hadn't been able to answer. *Did* she love Lucas? No, she didn't think so. She could, she realized, but that would have to come later. She was going to have to hurt before she was ready to love again, and she'd have to heal.

Not yet. *Maybe in the spring.*

But, God, Lucas was beautiful. He made her smile, and gasp, and feel substantial. He made her hungry. And he kept her safe, safe and protected in the blanket of his strong arms all winter long. For now, that was enough. He'd promised to keep her safe in winter, and Katie believed him.

When she finally made it back to the dock, she untied her boat and turned it back towards her tiny house. A pale glow shone in the still distant window that she knew looked into her kitchen. Her Lucas was probably there and warming something for dinner, something surprising. The fierce, icy northern wind blew stronger, and Katie was ready to be home.

Just then, a sudden and unexpected question leapt into her mind. Once it occurred to her, she couldn't imagine why she'd never thought to ask it before.

There was only one boat, and she was in it.

How on Earth had Lucas made it to and from the mainland without taking the boat?

8

Forgotten Things of Myth and Story

he days passed, one after another, each as unique and original as a snowflake. And yet, when Katie looked back on them, they all seemed rather the same, like the great and sudden mass of snowflakes in a winter storm. They piled one of top of another, until the individuality of each was lost in deep and icy drifts of endless white. May came and June followed, but winter's grip was cold and iron strong.

Nothing changed. Spring did not come.

Sometimes, late at night, the questions that had bothered Katie at New Sam's Pub returned to trouble her again, but by day they were numbed to silence. For the most part, Katie didn't worry about art and identity, or about love and hurt. She continued, and the days passed, one like another. That was enough. The motions of her existence became patterns, like the steps in a dance, or the crystalline angles of a snowflake. The monotony was comfortable and safe; winter was a womb.

She thought about the other question, too, the one she hadn't dared ask. She thought about how Lucas had come to and from the island without a boat. She never asked. Some wise part of her knew better. She buried the question deep, in the cold place in her heart where the need to make slumbered like a seed in the snow.

Lucas made a sled, and they went to the mainland to try it out. It flew down the slopes like a cannonball. They laughed until they couldn't breathe. Then they gasped, pulled the sled again to the top of the hill again, and laughed some more. Lucas promised to make some skis—he was handy with wood—and teach her how to soar over the snow like a bird. Katie smiled.

One night, they sat together on the sofa listening to the tingling sounds of snowfall. Lucas had made warm cocktails that tasted like butterscotch and bourbon. Katie was tired that night. She didn't want to talk, or read, or even watch TV. She just wanted to be close to Lucas, to sip her sweet drink and breathe his scent: sandalwood, salt, and flannel. She snuggled close, and he wrapped his warmth around her like a feather blanket.

"I love you," Lucas said.

Katie smiled. She wanted to cry. She opened her mouth but found she had no answer to give him in return. Instead, she kissed him, deeply, deeply, drinking him like the ocean drinking the rain. Lucas didn't seem to mind.

On a bright morning in early June when Lucas was away on a job, Katie found herself standing once again just inside the door of her studio, gazing in. She didn't enter. The shapes and shadows seemed distant and unfamiliar. She'd become a stranger there, she realized, a tourist in an unfamiliar place without a map. She no longer belonged in her own studio. The dust that had fallen over the stones and blocks of plaster was now as deep as a snowdrift. The forms inside them were lost; their silent voices no longer called to her. She thought about dusting. She didn't bother.

As she stood there, staring at the now unknown room, the questions fell upon her again, sudden and heavy in their unanticipated intensity.

Who am I? she wondered. *Oh God, who am I?*

No answers came.

She stood there, numb and staring, until, much later, Lucas came at last and pulled her, gently, away. He held her as a dancer would—his left hand held her right one high, and his right hand slid around her waist. They spun and stepped away, light as feathers, giggling like children and hearing secret music, and the door swung shut behind them.

That night they laughed and cooked dinner together, and then they played their peculiar games with stories and the chess pieces. But later, as Lucas slept with his chest pressed close against her back and his arm around her, the questions returned like wind to haunt the strange rooms of Katie's thoughts. They troubled her and kept sleep at bay.

Why can't I make anything?

Who am I?

No answers came, and the night passed, silent and still. Sleep took her at last, fitfully, in the final, darkest hours just before the pale morning.

As she dreamed, Katie found herself wandering through an attic, old and dusty. The questions nagged her even as she dozed, and the answers became secrets hidden away and forgotten. She searched, tugging at boxes and pulling away sheets, because she thought she'd left them somewhere near, shut behind attic doors, long before. But the doors were hidden and the keys were lost, and even if she found them it would be no good, because her fingers were too numb to work the locks.

She awoke, sobbing, at dawn, but Lucas was there to soothe her. She shivered, and he tightened his arms around her body as she cried.

"Shhh." His voice was soft and his breath was warm in her ear. "Sleep, sleep. It's early yet, sweet. I'm here to

protect you, remember? Just sleep, my heart. I won't let you hurt."

Lucas held her, the way winter hugs the world, and Katie remembered a story he'd told her once, about how Eskimos bury themselves in snow to survive when they're lost or trapped far from home in a storm.

"I don't know what to do," Katie whispered after a while. She always whispered in bed, even when there was no one close to hear.

"Sleep." Katie could hear the soft smile in his voice. "Love me."

I can't, Katie thought without speaking. *I don't know who I am.*

Three days later, Katie watered the two small plants she kept in her kitchen, and the tall one next to her sofa. The ones in the kitchen were supposed to have flowered, but they hadn't. They hadn't grown, not an inch.

Katie frowned and felt her brow crinkle. *I must be doing something wrong.* The plants hadn't changed at all. They hadn't even lost a single leaf.

That's not right. How can something be alive if it doesn't change or grow?

Once when Lucas was away, Katie went into her studio, determined to start something new. She forced herself, like a blindfolded prisoner facing a firing squad.

A painting—that would be simpler than sculpture, sure-ly. Or maybe just a quick sketch or two, something to flex the muscles. Anything.

For a moment, she thought the old feelings stirred in her again, like life quickening in her belly. She moved forward like a woman in a dream, slowly, her feet step-ping lightly on the cold, rough stone of the floor, toward white and empty canvases.

When she got there, she didn't find stories or shapes, or figures longing for the touch of color to free them from their chains of unbeing. She found agony instead, the fire of change lurking like danger, waiting to con-sume her, and she jerked her hands away.

Lucas came home that night and found her on the stone floor, curled in a fetal ball, knees under her chin, weeping. He didn't say a word. Instead, he dropped down next to her and pulled her cold body against his. For a long time, he held her there, not speaking, and she let him soothe her to calm numbness again, changeless and safe.

June passed its zenith and began to wane. Katie and Lu-cas decided to make a snowman, but their collaboration deteriorated into a snowball fight before they'd even fashioned the first icy sphere for the base.

Katie got the worst of it. Lucas was quick and he had a knack for sneaking, tricking her and hitting her from where she least expected it. His throws were straight and strong. Katie dodged most of them, but one hit her square on the shoulder, splashing snow where her check was bare beneath her hood and above her woolen scarf. The cold made her gasp.

Her own throws were less fortunate; her snowballs sailed wide or fell short.

"You throw like a girl," Lucas teased her.

"I *am* a girl, if you haven't noticed."

"Oh, I've noticed," Lucas answered with a wide grin and a wink.

"Pig," Katie accused. Lucas laughed and launched another snowball in her direction. Katie ducked just barely in time, but her feet slipped, and she tumbled down on her back in the deep snow.

"You okay?" Lucas called out to her.

Katie didn't answer. She lay there, quiet and unmoving.

"Katie?" Lucas' smile vanished.

In a flash, Lucas raced to Katie's side and knelt beside her. Too late, he saw a hint of a smile form on her face. She grabbed him by the arm and pulled. He fell and landed hard in the snowbank. He turned but before he could recover, twin snowballs smacked him right in the face. Katie's smile widened to a grin, a smug one. He laughed so hard that he almost couldn't breathe.

"Meanie."

"Yup," Katie agreed with a smug grin. "Now we're even!" She beaned him with another snowball, one she'd hidden behind her back. "And now we're not."

"That," said Lucas, "is the oldest trick in the book. I should know; I wrote the book on tricks."

"It worked, didn't it?"

"That's because I *thought,*" said Lucas, "that it was beneath you."

Katie smacked him with another snowball. It was mostly powder; she'd been shaping it secretly while Lucas watched her face so it wasn't her best work. It was effective all the same. They both exploded with another fit of laughter. When they caught their breath at last, Lucas reached for Katie, and she let him pull her close.

"A tricky one," he said. "I love the tricky ones."

"Me, too," Katie said. It wasn't the same as saying she loved him, but it was something.

They embraced there in the snow, and the embrace became a kiss, deep and warming, and Katie felt her whole body tremble in response. When they stood, they left the shape of an angel pressed deep into the snow behind them.

Katie and Lucas went inside just long enough to change clothes and pour mugs of coffee, but when they went back outside, the last of the daylight had faded to shadow. So early in the day, and it was already as black as midnight. The old man in the pub—Jamie—was right: the days weren't growing longer at all. Winter lingered and the world slept. Lucas put his arm around Katie, and she rested her head on his shoulder. Together, they stood there and watched the stars and the aurora borealis blazing its rainbow of shimmering pastel light in the black and chilly northern sky.

"Tell me another story," said Katie. "About the Northern Lights.

"Demanding, aren't you?"

"I am, sir!"

"It'll cost you a kiss, bold woman."

"I'll pay gladly." She did.

"They used to say," said Lucas, "that the auroras are torches carried by spirits, kind spirits that are seeking the souls of people who have just died, so they won't get lost, so they can lead them over that abyss at the end of the world. There's a narrow pathway across that great chasm, you see, the path to the land of light and music, of brightness and plenty, where there is no more pain or suffering, and where everyone is whole and young and beautiful again. This is a place where only the dead and Raven can go. Everyone we've ever lost is there, waiting, waiting with those torches. Even the animals. They're waiting there to guide us. When they want to talk to us, those spirits, they make a whistling noise, a sort of a whisper, like the wind."

"Who can answer them?"

"The old people say there are some who can call the aurora, and converse with it. They can hear its whisper.

And Raven, too, of course. They can send messages to those they left behind, those spirits with the torches. They can call to the ones they love, through the aurora and its whispers."

"That's nice," Katie said. "But it's not really a story."

"I guess it's not at that. Do you want your kiss back?"

"I do indeed." She took it, drinking him deeply, and then she took another. "Interest," she explained.

"And here's your change," said Lucas, and he kissed her again.

After a time, they went back inside to make love, and then to snuggle under a thick blanket and let the warm golden light of the fire dance across their faces like a caress. Outside, their barely-begun snowman waited, abandoned, unformed and shapeless. By morning the wind and winter had erased their effort utterly, leaving only a swell among white swells, endless and unchanging.

Late the next afternoon, Lucas found Katie standing again in the doorway to her studio and sipping a mug of coffee. He put his arms around her waist and pulled her close so he could kiss the top of her head. Katie smiled and snuggled back close against him. He'd been outside, bringing in more firewood. He smelled of pine and snow and flannel. Katie liked that smell.

"Hello there, Pretty One." He was looking past her, into the studio. "Are you going to make something to-day?"

"No. No, I don't think so."

"Then why stand here?"

"I don't know," she admitted. "Got to stand some-where, I guess." She knew she sounded snappy and wished she didn't, but she didn't apologize.

"Ah. Well, then. Maybe tomorrow."

"I don't think so," Katie admitted.

"Do you want to?"

Do I?

"I don't know," she said at last. "Maybe I've forgot-ten how."

"Maybe that part of you's just sleeping."

"I don't know." Katie shrugged, and liked the way her shoulders felt when they moved against his chest. "Maybe. Sleeping, like the world in winter."

"Like the part that hurts," Lucas said softly.

"Yeah. Like that. It might be . . . I don't know. It might be the same part. I . . . I mean, yeah. I think so. The part of me that has to heal, I think maybe that's the part where the art comes from. Does that make any kind of sense at all?"

She felt him nod.

"But I don't know where that part is any more, Lu-cas."

"Resting."

Lucas was still looking where she was, into the studio.

I wonder what he sees there? I wonder if he sees what I see now? Or does he still see the unborn art?

She didn't ask him. A quiet moment passed.

"Just resting," Lucas said again. The certainty of his steady voice was a comfort.

"Maybe. I don't know. It used to be that whenever I came into my studio—wherever it happened to be—I could hear the art calling me, like . . . like drowning men calling out for help. That's how urgent it was. Do you see? I just about couldn't rest, or even sit still, until I'd chiseled away the base stone and freed the form trapped inside. But now it's all gone, Lucas. All I see is a whole bunch of rock and dust. It's all gone."

She didn't cry; she didn't ache with the loss. Her heart was still, numb. She was cold but she did not shudder.

"But if it's gone, isn't that okay? It means you won't hurt anymore. I mean, that's good, right?"

Katie didn't answer.

"The pain's gone, isn't it?"

"But that's just it," said Katie. "It's not gone. It hasn't healed at all. It's just . . . buried. Frozen. Like . . . like fish in a winter lake. That's not the same thing, is it?"

"I don't guess I know. But hey there, isn't that enough? Isn't it enough not to hurt, to suffer?"

"I . . . I don't think so," Katie said.

"Why not?"

"Because it's not being alive."

"But it doesn't hurt. I thought that's what you wanted."

"Me, too. But I think . . . I think eventually I'm going to have to. Oh God, Lucas!"

"Why is that?"

"Because otherwise, I'm going to lose something. Something important."

"What?"

"Me," she said. "Katie Mason. I'm losing who I am."

"Maybe you're becoming someone new."

"No," Katie said, shaking her head. "No, I'm not doing that, either. That would mean growing, evolving. You know? Changing into something new and creative. I'm just . . . going on. Continuing. You know? But I'm losing me, my . . . my self. My identity."

"Maybe you're not losing anything. Like I said, right? Maybe it's just sleeping. Remember? Like you said. Like the world in winter."

Katie had a vague sense that she should do something, that she should take some kind of action before the very essence of her was numbed away into unbeing. But what could she do? She was no raven to call the world awake at the dawn of spring. She had no power over winter, or cold, or lost things.

"But the world wakes up in spring," Katie pointed out. "And it looks like spring has forgotten us."

In the morning, Lucas held her. They lay together for a long time, skin against skin, not moving or talking, even though they both knew the other was awake.

"I wonder," Lucas said at last. "I wonder if it dreams."

"Mmmm?" Katie asked, her voice still cottony with sleep.

"The part of you that's sleeping," said Lucas. "The part that makes art. I wonder if it dreams?"

"I don't know," Katie said.

The next morning, Katie went outside, coffee mug cradled in her hands, steam rising like a cloud to meet the rising sun. She was looking for Lucas, who'd been out before she'd stirred. She found him climbing down the ladder from the roof, carrying his tools on a bag slung over his shoulder.

"You're up early," Katie accused.

"So I am. But guess what? I finished!"

"The roof?"

"What else? I fixed the broken part, of course, and then I fixed the parts that looked like they were ready to break. And then, well, I figured I might as well fix all the rest, so it'll all match. And before I knew it, well, I'd put on a new roof, hadn't I? Now my girl is just as safe as she can be, protected like a babe in the womb, like an Eskimo in an igloo, no matter what ol' man winter decides to throw at her."

"Wow, thanks!"

"Like I said. I have to earn my keep, don't I? Now then. Why don't you come see for yourself? Quick now, before the snow comes again and covers it all up."

"Up there? You mean, on the roof?"

"Where else? Can't see it from down there, now, can you?"

"I suppose not. But isn't it . . . uh, dangerous?"

"Not with me. I'll keep you safe. I'll always keep you safe, Katie. C'mon. Here, you go first. I'll follow behind you."

Katie started up, and when she reached the top, Lucas was there to steady her and help her step off of the ladder and onto the roof's gentle slope. The roof wasn't that high, not really—her house was very small—but all the same she felt like Neil Armstrong taking one small step onto a strange new world. Lucas had swept away the snow and ice. The wood was utterly dry and, to Katie's surprise (and relief) it wasn't slippery at all. There was no wind, no cloud to mar a startlingly blue sky. Everything else was white. Lucas stood behind her and held her while Katie turned around slowly, like a weathervane rooster. The world stretched out around her, still and white and vast as the sea, not really different but somehow new all the same, all gentle slopes, like a downy blanket hugging the curves of a sleeping woman's body. Katie gaped, and remembered, oh, remembered how beautiful her island was, how still, and how tiny.

Something stirred inside her then, moving, moving, something deep inside called, called, called by the stark, white, cold beauty of the world in winter. It had been a long time since she'd changed her perspective.

"That's why I like coming up here," said Lucas. "You see it, don't you?" Katie nodded. "I knew you would. The world's different from above, isn't it? Even just a little. Beautiful."

"Beautiful," Katie echoed.

"But look, I brought you to see your roof, didn't I? Look, Katie!"

Katie looked down, and felt her mouth fall open, making an O.

Lucas had replaced all the shingles with new ones, new shingles made of wood. "Don't worry," he assured her. "I treated 'em all. Primed and varnished, you bet. They'll last you, through all kinds of weather, and for a good long time, too."

Lucas had varnished the tiles, just as he'd said, but in different shades—some deep red like autumn leaves, some dark as the earth, some natural, the color of virgin wood. From the different shades he'd made patterns, shapes and textures that reminded her a little of the ones she'd seen in the native art in Mrs. Tallbear's store, but utterly unique. When she didn't look straight at them, those patterns, they seemed almost to move, like creatures lurking slow and deep beneath a cedar sea.

Lucas hadn't just repaired her roof; he'd made art. He'd made it for her.

"Oh, Lucas, it's wonderful!"

"I'm glad you like it."

"It's beautiful!"

"Like you."

"But no one will see it!"

Lucas shrugged. "You did, didn't you? Birds will, I reckon. Besides, does something have to be seen to be beautiful? Maybe it can just be. Isn't that enough? Don't you think?"

On midsummer's day, Katie saw that the wild called to Lucas once more. He was restless and eager, and all morning his eyes were dark and bright as they darted to the door and the small windows. The urge to wander had come upon him again with all its fierce and irresistible intensity. Katie knew that. Sitting close to him, she could almost feel it swelling in her own breast. He needed solitude and open spaces, at least for a while. She patted his leg. "You'd better get started, don't you think?"

He looked at her, his head tilted to the side, a half-formed smile on his too-beautiful face.

"Well, go on! *Shoo!* You're not the only one who has things to do, you know." She said that, even though she didn't. She could give gifts, too.

With a grin, he promised to be back home in time for supper.

Katie nodded. "I might go out too," she said slowly, as though trying the words on for size.

There was a need in her, too, she realized. It wasn't longing, exactly, or even an ache. Rather, it was an absence, a void. She explored it curiously, like a child probing the space where a lost tooth had been with her tongue. She found only emptiness where she was certain there should be something else. Something . . . something.

"After I finish my coffee. And the next cup. Maybe I'll go to town."

Lucas seemed almost surprised, but he recovered quickly and nodded, grinning, pleased.

"Have fun, my sweet." He kissed her lightly on the top of her head.

"You, too," said Katie.

Lucas paused before he left her, just for a second, as though there was something left to say, and in that moment, Katie almost asked him how he came and went without the boat.

She didn't.

For some reason she couldn't begin to explain, she was afraid to voice the question. No, she was more than afraid;

she was terrified to the core of every cell in her body. Fear filled her from the very soles of her feet to the ends of the last tangled strands of her hair. It was as if the words were a taboo that, if spoken aloud, would break some secret spell, making Lucas disappear forever like the last snow in springtime. It was silly: she knew that; but the instinctive fear was rooted deep in the dark places inside her, and it was no less severe for all the light Katie's rational thoughts shined there.

What good was reason? Nothing made sense anymore. It was June, but winter lingered, cold and unchanging, as though it intended to stay until seasons and the passing of time were forgotten things of myth and story, long vanished into the distant past.

The question froze in her throat, numbed to silence. Katie didn't speak, and wind pushed the moment away. Lucas was gone.

Less than an hour later, she pulled on her hood, gloves, and scarf and ventured outside. The cold was astonishing. It struck her at once, rattling her bones like wind chimes in a hurricane. She lowered her head and pushed forward with her eyes half closed, fighting the terrible, icy wind with every step. The boat was still there, tied at its dock. Katie freed it, started the motor, and turned it towards the mainland.

9

Near Christmas

atie found Maggie Tallbear puttering busily around behind the front counter in her general store. The older woman seemed tired, but she mustered the energy to call out a friendly greeting when she heard the door chimes jingle.

"Why, if it isn't Miss Katie! Hey there, Hon! Long time no see!"

Katie smiled as she entered and struggled with the wind to pull the heavy door shut behind her. "I haven't been to town much lately."

"So I've noticed." Mrs. Tallbear winked. "If I had a handsome man like that waiting for me back home, why, I might never open up this old store again!"

Katie blushed. "You know about that?"

"Lucas told me when he came to buy groceries. I'm delighted for both of you. Everyone 'round town loves him. I don't know him too well, but he seems like a good man, dear. 'Course, I don't know you all that well, either, so I'm just trusting my old woman's instincts, you understand. But you said you needed to heal up a little, and a pretty man can be good for what ails you. 'Specially when the trouble's a broken heart. So how are things going with you?"

Katie wasn't sure how to answer, so she decided to change the subject. On the small table at the back of the store, Mrs. Tallbear had set up a little Christmas tree, complete with silver and gold decorations and twinkling lights. Below, she'd arranged a little nativity scene. Above, twin stylized portraits of Raven hung on the wall, like jet-black angels watching over the shepherds and baby Jesus. Katie's brow crinkled. "Isn't it a little late for all the Christmas stuff?" she asked. "What's that all about?"

"Oh, that," said Mrs. Tallbear. "Well, the Inuit people believe that if a day has meaning, the day opposite it on the calendar also has significance. See? So since we celebrate Christmas in December, we celebrate Near Christmas in June. Personally, I think it also helps us remember that Christmas does more than mark the passage of time. It's something that's supposed to last and be a part of life all year 'round. Isn't that right?"

"Near Christmas." Katie smiled. "I like that. So if you miss Christmas, you get another chance."

"I suppose so, at that," Mrs. Tallbear agreed with a slow nod. "And with all this awful winter, it seems rather appropriate, don't you think? Even if it *is* June rather than December. Where's the dratted springtime, to say nothing of the blasted summer! I think Raven forgot us this year. The world's still asleep. They say Raven likes bright shiny things. Maybe he'll wander by and see them and remember to wake the world."

"Like in the story you told me."

"Besides, we need a little light in all this darkness, don't we? Every bit helps. It cheers me a little. And it's about damn time, don't you think?"

"That reminds me," said Katie. "Last time I was here, your store was closed. The note said you had a family emergency. I hope everything's okay?"

Mrs. Tallbear looked away, sadly. "No, not okay."

"Oh, I'm sorry!" said Katie. "Truly, I didn't mean to pry!"

Mrs. Tallbear smiled to show she appreciated the sympathy. "It's okay, dear. I've got a cousin laid up bad sick is all." Mrs. Tallbear wore a brave mask, but Katie saw pain in her eyes, terrible and heavy. "He's older than me, but we grew up together. He's like another brother to me. It's kind of you to ask."

"That's nice. That you're close, I mean."

"Family's a treasure." Mrs. Tallbear kept on fussing around behind the counter, finding tasks to keep her hands busy. "He's got a bad cancer, though. The deep kind, down in the bones. We thought we were going to lose him. The doctors said he wasn't going to last the night, so I closed up the store and hurried off to be there with him. That's important, you know. To be there." Katie nodded. Mrs. Tallbear forced a smile. "But old Ned, that's my cousin's name, he fooled 'em all. He didn't die."

"I'm so glad for you!"

Mrs. Tallbear stopped her fussing and turned to look Katie in the eye. "Well, I appreciate that, but I'm not sure it's such a good thing. Not if I'm being honest."

Katie frowned and shook her head. "I don't understand."

"Oh, don't get me wrong, I don't want my poor cousin to die," Mrs. Tallbear explained quickly. "And when he's gone, I'm going to miss him something terrible, more than I can say."

"But," prompted Katie.

"But," Mrs. Tallbear paused to wipe away a tear. "But he's not getting any *better*, Katie, and he's not letting go. It's like he's just . . . caught. He's suffering so, and it just tears me apart to see him hurting like that, day in and day out. Life's a blessing, every breath. But this . . . it's not life, Katie."

"Oh, no!"

"He's not healing, and he can't seem to let go and pass on to a better place where all his hurt will be soothed away. He's just continuing, on and on, lingering and suffering without hope or rest. People aren't meant for that."

"That's terrible," said Katie. "Oh, I'm so sorry!"

"I know, dear, and I appreciate that." Mrs. Tallbear turned back to her counter, looking for more tasks. "Like I told you, it's a kindness. Sometimes, people forget what a comfort the care and compassion of friends can be."

"What can I do to help you?"

"You've already done it, dear." Mrs. Tallbear managed another smile, but the weariness and sorrow never left her eyes. "After that, why, there's nothing else anyone can do, I reckon. It's this damn awful winter...."

"No spring," Katie said softly. "No changes."

"Just so." Mrs. Tallbear sighed. "The days aren't getting longer like they're supposed to. The ice doesn't melt. Spring is four months late. Here it is midsummer, and winter lingers, on and on, and every day is the same. One after another."

"But we need seasons, don't we?"

Mrs. Tallbear nodded. "We need to rest, but then we need to wake up and move on. That's what life means. But that's not happening, is it? Just more winter, and the world sleeps. Nothing changes; nothing grows. All the old people say Raven's forgotten us."

"Like in the story," Katie said again.

"They say old Raven's gotten distracted. He's forgotten what he's supposed to do."

"He didn't call the sun. Did he? He didn't wake the world. He let it sleep, so spring won't come. Winter will last and last, so the world can sleep."

Mrs. Tallbear shrugged. "Well, that's what my people say."

"Do you believe that?" Katie asked seriously.

"Lots of people 'round here do. I guess it makes about as much sense as anything these days. Maybe it takes an impossible story to explain impossible events. And every story points to something, you know. Something true and abiding."

"Maybe. Maybe so. I guess."

"But you never answered my question."

Katie blushed. "Which question?"

"How are things going with you?"

"I'm fine." Katie looked away. "Really. I suppose I'd better go ahead and pick out all my groceries and stuff...."

"You can talk and shop at the same time," Mrs. Tallbear pointed out. She seemed glad to have something to distract her from thoughts of her cousin, caught between life and death like a bug in ice, and the long, enduring winter. "And that wasn't much of an answer, now was it? How are you and Lucas? What's growing between you? How's the healing coming? And the art?"

"I haven't done much," Katie hedged. She tried to focus her attention on cans of soup and vegetables. She picked up a new variety of Campbell's. "Is this good? Have you tried it?"

"It's soup. They're all fine enough. Don't change the subject, dear."

"I don't know what to say. I just . . . I haven't done much of anything. I'm like your cousin, I guess. I've just kind of . . . continued. You know?"

"That doesn't sound too good."

"I know." Katie glanced back at the cans of soup. "But I don't know what to *do* anymore. About the art *or* the healing. I don't even know how to fall in love with Lucas. It's like I'm asleep, and I've forgotten how to wake up."

"Sounds like you need Raven too. Just like the world. You need to wake up."

"I guess. Maybe. I don't know. I wanted to keep sleeping, because I was so afraid of how much it was going to hurt when I woke up...."

"But we need seasons, don't we, dear? Even the ones that hurt. Even when they hurt so awfully."

"I'm so afraid," Katie said, her voice less than a whisper.

"Of what? Hurting? Or healing?"

Katie looked back at Mrs. Tallbear. "Maybe I'm afraid of what I'll be after I heal. I'll be someone else."

"We all change, Katie. That's part of being alive."

"What if I can't make art anymore?"

"Are you making art now?"

133

"Point," Katie acknowledged. "I'm not doing much of anything."

"I see. So what is it you're really afraid of?"

"I'm afraid...." Katie felt tears gathering and growing heavy behind her eyes. "I'm afraid I'm forgetting who I am." That was it: that was the emptiness she'd felt earlier. That was the need that made her leave her cocoon and come to town.

"Well that can't be," Mrs. Tallbear declared. "Why, you're Katie Mason!"

"That's just my name. It's not who I am."

"It's a good place to start. Names have power, you know. Let's see. Katie. That's short for Katherine, right? What does that mean?"

"Pardon?"

"Katherine. What does the name mean?"

Katie frowned again. "It means pure, I think." She'd looked it up in a baby name book once, but it had been a long time ago.

"That's certainly good," said Mrs. Tallbear. "Pure what? Goodness, maybe?"

"Ha! I doubt it."

"Well, what then? Pure vision maybe? That's good, isn't it? And we know what Mason means, don't we? Someone who shapes stones. So there you are. That's a good start, isn't it? You're Katie Mason. Pure. A shaper, a maker. That sounds like a fine person to be."

"Maybe that's who I'm supposed to be," said Katie. She shook her head. "I don't know if it's who I am. Not anymore."

"Like I said, it's a good start," said Mrs. Tallbear. "I think the rest is up to you."

Katie packed her groceries in her truck and started the drive back to her dock. Strange, uncomfortable thoughts stirred and troubled her drive. Mrs. Tallbear was right, she decided. She'd been asleep long enough. She needed seasons, even if she was so terribly, awfully afraid. It was time to face the pain that waited for her, so that she could move past it and, God willing, find some way to turn it into art.

It was time to wake. She'd been hiding in her chrysalis too long. It was time to remember who she was, and to discover who she was to become.

It was time to hurt.

Maybe Lucas can help, Katie thought. Even as the thought occurred to her, she knew, she knew with absolute certainty in a deep place in her heart, that it was true. Lucas *could* help. He could bring forth spring and summer within her, and the harvest of autumn. And if he did, the art would be amazing, beautiful and heart-rending beyond anything she'd ever dreamed.

But no, no. That wouldn't do.

If that art was going to mean anything, it had to come from within her. It had to be conceived in Katie's soul and born of her own hands. No one could help her, not even Lucas. Even if it hurt, even if the pain was beyond endurance, she had to do it herself. Even if it killed her, or, worse, even if it didn't and she had to deal with the agony of being alive. She had to be Katie, and she had to make.

Of course, that was a lot easier said than done. Katie had no idea how to begin. The world was asleep; seasons no longer changed. Winter's grip was strong, and the land was numb and frozen. It was like the story said. Raven had forgotten to wake the world.

Slowly, slowly, her numbness warmed. Her sleeping mind began to stir and stretch, sore from disuse. When she looked out at the sloping landscape around her, a still sea of endless white, she knew that, for the first time in an age, she was seeing with an artist's eyes.

Lucas can help, Katie thought again. He always seemed to understand, he always seemed to know what to say. Maybe....

Lucas. Oh God, Lucas.

Lucas, who came and went without using the boat. Who didn't mind heights, even when the icy wind was fierce. Who brought her pretty things and liked shining lights.

She tried to stop the chain of thoughts, oh she tried, but her waking mind was making her recognize things that her resting mind could comfortably ignore.

Sometimes Raven visits people, to see what the humans are up to. And when he does, he disguises himself as a man.

Lucas, who had said he'd keep Katie from hurting, who'd promised to keep her safe in winter.

Now sometimes, Raven forgets who he is. He forgets he's Raven.

The story said that sometimes, Raven forgets what he is supposed to do. Sometimes he forgets to wake the world, and spring doesn't come.

But no, no. It was impossible. Of course it was. It was just a story. Old stories aren't true, not literally. They point to truth, but they aren't history. They're metaphors, masks for deeper mysteries.

Aren't they?

But if that was so, why was the day midwinter-short on the summer solstice? Why hadn't the sun returned? Why hadn't the world awakened?

Names have power, Mrs. Tallbear had said. What did the name Lucas mean? Katie racked her brain, seeing herself flipping the pages of that long-ago baby name book. It was no good. She found her phone and hoped that, for once, she'd get at least one bar. She opened a browser and found a baby name site. She typed in the name Lucas in the search bar. *Light bringer.* She smiled, a subtle, gentle smile. Of course.

But what about his last name?

The smile vanished. No, no. She couldn't think like this. It was impossible. *Impossible!*

Wasn't it?

Impossible, like a winter that lingers through June. *Oh God, no. Please no.*

Katie tried to think about the situation logically, to examine all the angles as an educated woman of the new millennium should.

Stories are just stories!

Try as she might, she couldn't make the pieces fit together, at least not according to her old definitions of logic and reason. When reason failed, when one stepped beyond the limits of logic, one turned to faith. Katie knew that, or she had, once. Art is all about faith, even when the artist doesn't know what it means, or what she has faith *in*. The mystery is enough.

But faith is not a thing for the numb, for the asleep. It is a thing of light and life.

What if she was right? And what if, oh God! What if Lucas never remembered who he was? What if he never remembered his identity, his true self? Would it be lost, just like hers was? Would the world sleep forever?

What if she was right?

And she was right. She knew it. She knew it deeply in the heart.

Raven had tricked the world into long slumber, so that she could rest and not suffer. Raven, who loves the light, had left the world in darkness out of love for her. Raven. Lucas. He had forgotten. He had done it for her.

And what if he *did* remember? What then?

He would leave her, and spring could come, and Katie would hurt even more.

But at least she would remember who she was. Just like Lucas. She'd be Katie Mason, and if she managed to survive the terrible, searing pain, she'd begin to heal at last. And maybe, God willing, maybe she'd be able to make art again.

Suddenly, Katie realized that she'd already made her decision, almost before she'd been aware that she had one to make. She couldn't continue, safe in her chrysalis, while the world slept in eternal winter. The cost was too high, both for herself and for Lucas. It was time to wake. When the world is dark, the unknown light is the one that guides most truly.

She felt the doors in her brain opening, just a crack, and she felt the agony of the fires there reaching, at last, with terrible, glowing fingers to melt away her icy winter cocoon and burn her soul. She was hurting and afraid, already, and it hadn't really begun. The fear made her tremble as she drove.

Nonetheless, Katie knew what she had to do. It was going to be hard, so very, awfully hard. But she had to find courage, and she had to act. She already knew how to begin.

She had to go back, and she had to ask Mrs. Tallbear one last question.

And if the answer was what she thought, knew, it would be, she'd have some more shopping to do.

"Katie!" Mrs. Tallbear said. "Gracious me, this is a surprise! Did you forget something? I was just about to lock up and go home."

"I have to ask you something. It's important."

Mrs. Tallbear tilted her head, puzzled. "Of course, dear. What is it?"

"Tulukkam," said Katie. "What does it mean?"

"Why, that's Lucas's last name, isn't it?"

"That's right," said Katie, nodding. "But I mean the word. You said names are important. Please, what does it mean?"

"It's an old Inuit word," Mrs. Tallbear said. "It's the Inuit word for raven."

Mrs. Tallbear was confused, but she was wise enough not to ask questions. Instead, she simply helped Katie find the things she needed. When the new purchases were packed in the truck, Katie hurried back to her dock as quickly as the icy road conditions would allow.

When she reached her boat, she didn't take it back to her house. Instead, she turned it north. Sikrinaktok Island wasn't far, not very far, anyway. She went there. She went to Sikrinaktok Island, the place in Mrs. Tallbear's story. The place where, each year at midwinter, Raven went to wake the world.

She steered around the unfamiliar island until— *yes!*—she found the remains of an old dock, still usable, if barely.

She took a deep breath for courage, and then she counted slowly to three. There was no turning back.

I'm Katie Mason, she told herself. *I'm Katie Mason, dammit. I can do this.*

The island was bare; there were no houses, not even a tree. There was only ice. Ice and snow and rock, winter's very heart, until the island met the blue and foaming motion of the sea. That was okay. Ice was what Katie needed.

She started to work.

She went back to Sikrinaktok Island the next day, too, and again on the day after that. She stayed from first light to long after dark. When she left to go home each night, her hands were raw and bleeding.

10

All Is Calm and Bright

t was June Twenty-fourth, Near Christmas Eve. That night, Katie realized that she did, in fact, love Lucas, that she loved him more deeply and truly than she'd ever loved before. How could she not have known that? Maybe because love was a thing for the awake, or the waking, for those brave enough to hurt. That was when she understood what love is, the art of gently leading someone back to themselves when they've forgotten the way. Lucas had done that for her; it was his dearest gift.

Katie held Lucas more tightly than she'd ever held a man, because she knew that tomorrow, she would have to let him go. If Lucas noticed, he gave no sign. He slept soundly in her arms, and he didn't wake when she cried.

Lucas left the next morning, Near Christmas Day, saving her the trouble of thinking of an excuse to send him away. He promised to be home in time to help make supper, and Katie smiled back at him. As soon as he was gone, she got busy.

First, she bundled up and went outdoors, where as far as she could see, the world was stark and white, frozen and still. Walking carefully so she wouldn't slip on the icy stones, she made her way down to the dock where her boat was tied. There, she retrieved the last packages she'd brought from Mrs. Tallbear's store and kept hidden under the seat. It took three trips, but one by one she carried them all inside.

She had to hurry. Lucas wouldn't be back for several hours, but she had a lot to do. As she worked, she hummed her favorites carols to herself: *Silent Night*, *Ave Maria*, and *O Holy Night*. When she cried, she told herself it was because the songs carried memories, happy and sad, of times long past, of things that were lost and people who were gone.

When she was finished at last, she put on her necklace of pearls, and they sparkled like a constellation.

Lucas returned to a house transformed. As always, dozens upon dozens of candles were scattered throughout every room, but everything else was different. A tiny

Christmas tree stood in the corner of the main room, right next to the fireplace. It was artificial, but, adorned with shiny ornaments hung amid a sparkling constellation of twinkling white lights, it was lovely to behold all the same. Sparkling decorations hung from the rafters and the cupboards. Boughs of holly and tinsel with sparkling lights draped the walls.

Lucas's dark eyes opened wide, and as he turned, Katie could see the light of the candles reflected there, like stars shining in a perfectly clear winter's night sky, when all is calm and bright. His mouth made an O.

As Katie watched, he turned. Every wall, every corner was decorated with green garlands, red ribbons, and bright ornaments, silver and gold, the shiny things

Raven loves, sparkling in the light of the candles, all of them. Even Katie's studio was no longer still and dark. In less than a day, she had turned the drab, gray walls into a miracle of light and color, bright as the sky. Lucas turned slowly, and when at last he turned back to Katie, bright tears were shining in his eyes.

"Oh, Katie," he said. "Why? Why did you do this?"

Katie managed a smile through her own tears. "To celebrate a virgin girl who gave birth to a little baby boy on a cold winter morning, a boy who came to bring light to the world." Just like Mrs. Tallbear said, a story that has resonance and meaning in every corner of the world. Even this one.

"Katie—"

"Shhh." Katie stepped close to him and held a finger to his lips. "You remember, don't you?"

He kissed her finger, gently, before he spoke. "I remember."

"You know who you are now, don't you?"

"I know."

"It's been too long," Katie said. "The world's been asleep. You have to go wake it up."

"But Katie, my dear, sweetest Katie, I did it for you! I forgot, so that I could love you, and keep you safe. You said you were going to hurt, you were going to hurt when spring came—"

"I know, my heart, I know."

"I don't want you to suffer."

"I know. Oh God, I promised myself I wasn't going to cry! But Lucas, my Lucas, I think I have to. You see, I'd forgotten who I am, too. Now it's time for me to wake up and remember. And If I can't, well, then it's time to find something else I can be. Something new and creative."

"I wanted . . . I wanted us to stay here forever." Lucas cried too. "I wanted us to love each other, and I wanted us to be safe and never hurt."

"I know, my heart, believe me I know. But that can't be. You have to be alive to love. Don't you see? When I can't feel pain, I can't feel anything. And to love, I have to embrace all that you are with all that I am. I have to commit totally and give completely. But I can't do that; I can't do that when I'm numb. I can't do it when I don't know who I am."

"Katie—"

"Oh God, Lucas. Oh God! I'm so scared!"

Lucas took her in his arms and held her close.

"I don't know what's going to happen," he said.

"I know. Me either."

"When I change . . . sometimes . . . sometimes I forget."

"I know. That's why we have to hang up all these decorations, right? To remind you who you are so you can come back and wake up the world."

"I might not be able to come back to you."

"I understand."

"I'll try to!"

"I know."

"But Katie, my Katie, what will happen to you?"

"I'm going to wake up," she said. "I'm going to hurt."

"And if I can't come back, if I forget—"

Katie buried her face in the wool of his sweater. It was rough and warm against her cheek. "That will hurt too."

"Then I've only made things worse, haven't I?"

"Never that." She managed to smile a little, even though Lucas couldn't see it. "No, my dearest, never that. It'll hurt, but I'll get through it. I'll heal, Lucas. It'll be slow, but someday, oh, someday I'll be whole again. I will! And then I'll remember you, and I'll treasure all the time we had together, and all the gifts you gave me. You were my miracle, Lucas, my love, and you came to me when I needed one most."

"Will you . . . will you make art again?"

"I don't know," Katie admitted. She lifted her face and met his gaze. "Maybe. I hope so. Someday."

Lucas smiled and reached out to caress Katie's cheek. His eyes were sad. Katie took his hand in hers and kissed the tips of his fingers. They were quiet for a long time. They held each other, tightly, and for those all-too-fleeting moments, the cold seemed far away.

"I love you, Katie," said Lucas. "Of all the shining things, you are the brightest. But I have to wake the world."

"We need seasons," Katie agreed. She held him close again.

"Oh my heart, I have to go now."

Katie nodded without moving her face from his chest.

"I know," she said. "To Sikrinaktok Island."

"Good-bye, my love," said Lucas.

"Good-bye, dear, sweet Lucas. My love. You brought light to my life. Go to Sikrinaktok Island. I left you something there. A present. Please, enjoy it for a moment or two, and try to remember me if you can."

When Lucas reached the island, he found Katie's gift. She'd made a sculpture out of ice—a single feather as tall as Lucas himself, shining like crystal, bright where it caught the last of the pale evening sun.

For a long moment, Lucas stood there, marveling at its perfect and fleeting beauty. He cried again, because he knew that when he called the sun, Katie's gift, her Raven's feather, would melt and be lost. He cried for Katie, and for things that are lovely but fade with the passage of time and seasons.

At last he bowed his head. Then he changed.

Lucas's body grew smaller, and night-black feathers fell across him like a shadow. Then he gave a great Ga! Raven called to the sun, and he took to the sky. He circled once, twice, and then he was gone.

The light grew brighter and tears of moisture beaded the surface of Katie's ice feather. As it dwindled, each shining drop caught golden light and shattered it, brightly, brilliantly, into all the infinite colors of the rainbow.

Raven likes shiny things.

Spring came, and summer followed fast on its heels. Time passed.

In her little house, Katie hurt with agony so intense she thought it would shred her very soul. She wept and screamed and bled, and then she was utterly and desperately silent for long periods before the awful cycle started all over again. But after a time, she began, at last, the long, slow process of healing. She cried less, and less after that, and now and then she smiled. The pain was terrible, but she was Katie Mason, and someday she would be whole again.

Sometimes she found the ladder and climbed to the roof, sweeping off Lucas's shingle art and sitting down, letting the varnished shapes swim and breathe, letting the beauty of a waking, changing world surround her like a blanket or a hug. Sometimes she watched the aurora borealis from there, from her place on the roof Lucas had made for her and listened for their whispers. Once she brought her sketchbook as she climbed, but she didn't open it. It was enough to hold it, safe like a seed in the ground.

Sometimes she stood in the doorway of her studio and looked in at the white blocks and tools waiting for her there in the darkness. She didn't go in. The ice sculpture for Lucas had been a start, but it wasn't time for art. No. Not yet, not yet. Spring was a time for waking; perhaps the time for harvest would follow in time, a season of deep color and plenty, an autumn of the heart. Maybe it was like loving again. Maybe it would be time again soon. Or someday.

Maybe.

Or maybe not.

In any case, things were changing. The world was awake at last. Ice flowed to rivers, and rivers met the sea. For the time being, that was enough. Katie moved through her tiny house with the light steps of the newly reborn.

Now and then, Katie thought she heard the echo of silent voices calling to her from hidden figures trapped in stone. She listened carefully, but the sounds were faint and distant, like the voices of a dream lost upon waking. Maybe it was art waiting to be born, or maybe it was just the sound of ice melting. Maybe it was simply the music of rushing water.

Katie listened. Time would tell.

She didn't have the heart to take the Christmas decorations down, not right away. They were lovely and they cheered her. They reminded her of rebirth and time, and the turning of seasons.

Every night she lit candles. If Lucas was coming, they would lead him home. If not, well, at least they pushed back the darkness a little. Then, when her house was filled with flickering, golden light, Katie put on her necklace of pearls, stark and perfect white: not cold like ice, but bright and shining, like guiding stars.

"In the depth of winter, I finally learned that within me there lay an invincible summer."

— Albert Camus

About the Author

After a 30-year career in new media, where his titles have included VP, Digital Media, VP, Creative, Executive Producer, and even CEO, John Adcox is now concentrating on storytelling. In addition to his writing, he is the CEO of Gramarye Media, Inc., the "next generation" book publisher, game developer, and movie studio of the future. More of his books are coming soon. You can learn more about them at http://johnadcox.com/.

About the Illustrator

Carol Bales studies, works, and teaches in a place where technology and creativity intersect. Educated in painting at the University of Tennessee and Human-Computer Interaction at Georgia Tech, she works as a senior User Experience Researcher for The Weather Company and teaches at Georgia State University.

The couple lives in Atlanta, Georgia.